CONFEDERATES DON'T WEAR *couture*

CONFEDERATES DON'T WEAR *couture*

BY STEPHANIE KATE STROHM

GRAPHIA
Houghton Mifflin Harcourt
Boston New York 2013

 Published in the United States by Graphia,
an imprint of Houghton Mifflin Harcourt Publishing Company.

www.hmhbooks.com

The text of this book is set in Garamond.
Book design by Carol Chu

Library of Congress Cataloging-in-Publication Data
Strohm, Stephanie Kate.
Confederates don't wear couture / by Stephanie Kate Strohm.
p. cm.
Sequel to: Pilgrims don't wear pink.
Summary: While touring with a group of Confederate Civil War re-enactors for a summer internship, Libby and Dev attempt to design and sell Southern Confederate costumes for a ball, investigate haunted battle grounds, and seek handsome Southern soldier boys.
ISBN 978-0-547-97258-9
[1. Interpersonal relations—Fiction. 2. Friendship—Fiction.
3. Historical reenactments—Fiction. 4. Clothing and dress—History—
19th century—Fiction. 5. Haunted places—Fiction. 6. Internship programs—Fiction.
7. Confederate States of America—Fiction.]
I. Title. II. Title: Confederates don't wear couture.
PZ7.S9188Con 2013
[Fic]—dc23 ISBN 978-0-547-97258-9

Manufactured in the United States of America
DOC 10 9 8 7 6 5 4 3 2 1
4500406842

*For Max—you are the Darcy
to my Elizabeth, the Rhett to my
Scarlett, and the Emmett to my Elle.*

prologue

"Ah! Mr. Yankee!" I read. "If you want to know what an excited girl can do, just call and let me show you the use of a small seven-shooter and a large carving-knife which vibrate between my belt and my pocket, always ready for emergencies."

Whoa. This Sarah Morgan Dawson was no simpering Southern belle. I tucked a few blond curls behind my ear and kept reading. I couldn't believe I'd stumbled upon this treasure trove of nineteenth-century Southern diaries. The University of North Carolina had digitized them, and they felt like my own personal window to the past, just a few clicks away.

A cloud of Gucci Pour Homme so thick I could almost see it swirled into the library, heralding the arrival of my favorite person at St. Paul Academy: my best friend, Dev.

"*Who's* the cutest girl in the library?" Dev boomed as he flung his skinny frame into the seat across from me, propping his chunky black motorcycle boots up on the wooden table. "Only Mother Nature can do highlights like these, people!"

He may have been a totally genius fashion designer and the best BFF a girl could ever ask for, but he still hadn't mastered the concept of the inside voice.

"Okay, one, feet off the table—that's just rude." I tapped his boot with my pink glittery gel pen until he removed it. "Two, I just found this *amazing* Civil War diary online, and I do not want to be distracted right now; three, this is a library, so shhh," I admonished Dev. "And, four," I concluded, "what on earth are you doing in here? I've never seen you in the library. Not once. Not ever. Not since you were stopped at the door freshman year for having a contraband iced caramel macchiato. So what on earth could possibly bring you in here?"

"That's how you *know* it's important. Because only something serious could bring me back to this iced-coffee desert of freakish silence," he insisted. "Hey, you're wearing the kilt I made you!" he noticed excitedly.

In addition to supplementing my school uniforms, Dev had turned exploiting the loopholes in the St. Paul Academy dress code into an art form. Sure, they said boys had to wear black or gray pants, but they never said they couldn't be suede. Today he wore a distressed black blazer over a sheer white shirt tucked into skintight leather pants; his striped uniform tie hung loosely around his neck.

"You look kind of like a preppy rock 'n' roll pirate," I told him.

"Libby!" Dev clapped his hands together with glee. "You just *get* me. Skirt looks great, btw. And speaking of exquisite tailoring," he continued, "you remember the jaw-droppingly chic ensembles I pulled together for your little shindig last summer?"

"Of course," I said, nodding. "How could I forget?"

They had been truly magnificent. Last summer, when I worked as an intern at Camden Harbor's Museum of Maine and the Sea, Dev had made the most beautiful historical costumes imaginable for the end-of-the-season costume ball. It was a total dream come true: I'd finally felt like I'd jumped back in time, like I'd been able to really live history. Sure, not everyone dreams of cast-iron cookware and corsetry, but it had been the perfect summer for me.

"So, naturally, I've been thinking about the success of my colonial couture," he said, stroking his chin, "and while I had never intended to be a historical fashion designer, I must admit, there are certain advantages. Some of it is very appealing: Exaggerated silhouettes. Huge skirts. Over-the-top fabulousness. I mean, hello!" He sat up very straight. "I am over-the-top fabulous!"

"That you are," I agreed.

"So, naturally, it was a very small step from colonial couture to . . ." He held up two flailing jazz hands. "Confederate Couture! Ta-da!"

"Ta-what-now?" I asked, confused.

"Confederate Couture!" he repeated, more enthusiastically.

"Do Confederates even *wear* couture?" I asked skeptically. "And I'm really trying to read right now."

"Ba baaaaaaaaaa ba baaaaaaaaaaaaaa," he sang grandly, to the tune of the theme song from *Gone with the Wind*. "We're gooooooooooooooooing soooooooooooouth."

"Shhh!" A very angry girl in oversize hipster headphones looked up from her computer and tried to incinerate us with a glare.

"Can we sing along later?" I asked. "This diary I'm reading is *really* cool! I promise. Seriously. Listen." I *had* to read him what I'd found. I was always trying to get Dev more interested in history, and this might just be dramatic enough to spark his interest.

"What did you say it was—some girl's diary? Snooze."

"Um, hello, no snooze at all." I read him the quote I'd found, and from the moment I read "Mr. Yankee," he did seem to perk up considerably. "See? Cool, right? There are actually a lot of misconceptions about women in the antebellum South. Lots of them went hunting and fishing, participating in what we think of as stereotypically masculine pursuits. I mean, look at what a badass Sarah Morgan was! They weren't all sitting around, flirting and fluttering their fans."

"Nothing wrong with flirting. But my belt *could* use a carving knife," Dev said contemplatively. "Why are you so into this diary, anyway?"

"Well, this is the closest I'll ever get to experiencing the Civil War, right? To really understanding what it would have been like for a girl my age to live through that."

"Hmmm." Dev stroked his chin methodically, the fluorescent lights glinting off his perfectly buffed nails. "What if there was a way for you to *actually* live through the Civil War?"

"Keep talking."

"This is what I've been *trying* to tell you, Libby!" he said, sighing with exasperation. "Have you heard of this Civil War reenactment thing? You know, like in *Sweet Home Alabama*?"

"Of course I've heard of it. I've even met some people who do it."

"Eeuw, really?" Dev made a disgusted face. "Super lame. It's, like, almost as bad as LARP-ing. People running around, having fake battles, and pretending to be soldiers. Wearing uniforms they never wash and eating something called 'hardtack,' which is not as much fun as the name might first lead you to believe."

"It's really not that lame! It's cool," I countered. "People take these reenactments very seriously. This is about as close to total historical accuracy as you can get."

"Total historical accuracy: the Libby Kelting dream," he said, smirking. "Hence, *we* are going south. I've already rented a sutler's tent with the Fifteenth Alabama Volunteer Infantry!"

"What's a sutler?"

"Oh, Libby, I'm disappointed." He shook his head. "Who's the history nerd now? A sutler is a civilian merchant who sells provisions to an army in the field, in camp, or in quarters." He smiled like the cat that had just caught the canary.

"I don't know everything." I blushed.

"I know that you don't know everything. I just never thought I'd get you to admit it." He grinned. "Anyhoo, sutlers set up tents at reenactments and sell stuff—hats, clothing, canteens, what have you. And let me tell you, these reenactors are *super* specific about their uniforms." He rolled his eyes. "Beyond boring! No creative license! Everything has to be exactly the same as it was back then, down to the thread count and button holes. So naturally, I decided to cater to the ladies—because even civilian reenactors deserve to look fabulous! So we'll be selling ball gowns, tea dresses, day dresses galore! All at Dev's Confederate Couture. I scored us a super-sweet gig, following around the Fifteenth Alabama, giving them a *very* minor percentage of the profits in exchange for transportation to the battlefields and a tent."

"Let me get this straight: You want to go to Civil War reenactments and sell nineteenth-century women's costumes." I gave him my best skeptical look. "Do you *have* nineteenth-century women's costumes?"

"I have something better," he said smugly. "Connections. You remember my uncle Raza?"

"The one you stayed with in New York last summer?"

"Yes! He has a sari store in Murray Hill and mad connections in the Garment District. So he's gonna hook us up! Bargain prices on top-quality fabrics. We'll make a few samples, take measurements, and have our clients fill out order forms. Easy-peasy. I'll sew 'em when we get back. Custom Confederate Couture. So pack your bags! We are ready to go, baby!"

"I don't know if I'm ready to go," I said doubtfully.

"Libby, you're my model. I neeeeed you," he whined. "To model my fashions. Did you not hear what I just said about specializing in women's wear? Plus, you can deal with all the boring nerd stuff. Lend me some nice historical accuracy. Cute sticker," he said, tapping the pink cupcake on the back of my computer.

"Oh, Dev, I don't know. I—"

"Stop protesting. I have a beyond-perfect business model. What are your concerns?"

"Your mom's okay with this?" I asked skeptically. "With you rolling around Alabama totally unsupervised?" Dev's parents were pretty strict, and Dev could find a way to get into trouble at a maximum-security prison run by nuns.

"Libby, we're mere *months* away from college. To put it plainly, our lives are basically no longer supervisable. It's time for us wee baby birds to fly from the nest. Besides, both my parents applauded my ingenuity and economic ambition," he said, preening. "And your mom's fine with it too."

"What? How do you know that?"

"Duh, I called her. You know I always enjoy a good chat

with Mrs. K. And she gave you the go-ahead. I only had to *slightly* exaggerate the adult supervision factor." He flashed me a thumbs-up. "All the mommies are onboard. We're ready to roll."

"Wait a minute, I'm still not—"

"Don't even pretend you don't want to go." He picked up a pen and starting doodling stars in my margins. "You were waxing rhapsodic about the charms of olden times like two seconds ago."

"Well, yes, I mean, it would be amazing to go," I said somewhat wistfully. "But . . . I had planned to spend the summer with Garrett and—"

"Don't play the boyfriend card," he interrupted. "Don't you dare. First of all, I'm not even sure someone who lives six states away even qualifies as a boyfriend."

"Hey!" I protested. "That's so not fair. We talk every day!"

"Okay, you have an electronic pen pal that you made out with a couple times." Dev rolled his eyes. "Congratulations."

"Just because you don't believe in long-distance relationships—or relationships, for that matter," I amended, as Dev glared, "doesn't mean they can't work out."

"Fine, boyfriend, pen pal, whatevs." Dev held up his hands in surrender. "It all boils down to this: Do you want to go to the Civil War, yes or no?"

"Yes," I admitted.

"Then your cerebral swain will understand, I promise you. If I know geek boy, he'll start spouting off about intellectual opportunities and chasing the dream or something."

"Well . . ." I hemmed and hawed. "I have to at least talk to him about it."

"Thought you might say that." Dev nimbly swiped my computer, turned it to face him, and banged on the keyboard until my laptop started emitting a shrill ring.

"You can*not* use a phone in here!" I whisper-screamed, horrified.

"This place has *so* many rules," Dev complained. "And it's not a phone."

Before we got kicked out of the library, I managed to hustle Dev and my ringing computer into the relative safety of the adjacent computer lab. It was empty except for a group of guys clustered in the corner playing World of Warcraft. As soon as Dev slid the computer onto an empty table, the screen filled with the face of my boyfriend, Garrett McCaffrey.

He looked just like he did almost a year ago when he'd pulled me out of an apple barrel: unruly dark hair, thick plastic-framed Clark Kent glasses, and an adorkable comic-book T-shirt. I still couldn't believe it had taken me an entire summer to realize that he was the Mr. Darcy to my Elizabeth Bennet. How could I *ever* have thought he wasn't totally cute and the only boy for me? I must have had a fit of temporary insanity. It may have taken a ghost, *Northanger Abbey*, and a nineteenth-century whaling vessel to bring us together, but at least I'd come to my senses eventually.

"Libby!" Garrett said happily, his eyes crinkling as he smiled. "This is a surprise. Good timing. Just got back from soc class." His look changed to confusion as Dev pushed his way into the frame. "Uh . . . hi, Dev."

"Do you think I need cheek implants?" Dev stared into the tiny camera, massaging his face. "I think this camera makes my cheeks look weird."

"Your cheeks are fine." I resumed my place in front of the camera as Dev started ensuring that his gelled hair was perfectly spiked. "And, Garrett, your cheeks are perfect."

Garrett laughed and leaned back in his chair, stretching his long arms. I could see a sliver of dorm room in the frame behind him, just as messy as it had been the couple of times I'd visited him at Tufts.

"'Mutant and Proud,'" Dev read off Garrett's *X-Men* T-shirt. "Oh, Garrett." He sighed. "Didn't you get that Marc Jacobs gift card I sent you for your birthday?"

"Yeah!" Garrett nodded happily. "I got some great socks."

I stifled a giggle as Dev's face fell.

"Listen, I'm glad you called. I mean, face-chatted," Garrett said seriously, straightening his glasses.

"Libby needs to talk to you about the summer!" Dev shrieked before I swatted him away.

"Uh, before you say anything about the summer"—Garrett started rustling around in his desk drawer—"I want to show you something." He produced a stack of papers and brochures.

"Does that say 'the Paul Revere House'?" I asked, squinting.

"Yeah." He nodded. "The thing is, I got that internship at the *Boston Globe*—"

"YOU GOT IT?!" I screamed happily.

"Shhhhh!" the World of Warcraft guys admonished me. Dev stuck his tongue out at them.

"Garrett! You got it!" I continued, more quietly. "Oh my God, I'm so happy for you!"

"Thanks." He blushed and looked even more adorable. "I know we were going to spend the summer together in Maine. And I want to spend the summer with you. But—"

"But you have to take it," I interrupted him. "Garrett, you have to! This is your dream internship. Your churning butter in a hoop skirt, if you will."

"Well, I probably won't describe it like that, but, yeah, it is," he said, laughing. "Which is why I got you these!" He held up his stack of papers triumphantly. "The Paul Revere House, the Commonwealth Museum, the Gibson House Museum. All in Boston; all still accepting internship applications!"

"If you love something, let it go," Dev whispered. "Let it go to Alabama."

"Alabama?" Garrett asked, his brow furrowing. He may have had terrible eyesight, but he had excellent hearing.

"The thing is—" I started to say.

"The thing is I've found an opportunity for Libby to follow her dreams," Dev interrupted. "To follow them all the way to a Civil War reenactment. The Olympics of living history."

"Dev wants me to sell ball gowns with him at Civil War reenactments. Down south," I explained.

"Oh," Garrett said, and I could see him deflate a little bit. "That sounds pretty cool. I mean, these Boston museums are good too . . . but they're not living history. You'd probably have to help out in the gift shop or something . . ."

"But we could be together!" Obviously, I would much rather spend my summer wearing a hoop skirt in a Civil War camp than working in a gift shop, but I'd really been looking forward to being with Garrett all summer. I'd visited him a couple of times at Tufts, and he'd come out to St. Paul on one of his breaks and had another trip planned out here for prom, but it really wasn't the same as being together for three whole months, all day, every day. But to live in Civil War reenactments for the summer . . . The hoop skirts were swishing and swirling in front of my eyes . . . and . . . and . . .

"Garrett, let me speak to you, mano a mano," Dev sniffed, and smooshed his head against mine. "I need her. For just a few itty-bitty months. And then I'll deliver her safe and sound to the great state of Massachusetts, where you can spend the entire academic year, slash the rest of your lives, together."

I elbowed him in the ribs.

"I think you should go," Garrett said decisively, folding up the brochures. "This reenactment thing sounds like something you'd really love. Plus the costume opportunities will be way better." He smiled, and I did too. "Besides, the Paul Revere House will be here next year."

"You're sure?"

"Sure," he said softly. "I love you, Libby."

"I love you too," I answered.

"VOMIT!" Dev shrieked, and closed the laptop.

"Shhh!" the WoW nerds in the corner chorused. Dev rolled his eyes yet again.

"That was rude! I didn't get to say goodbye!"

"It's good to keep 'em on their toes." Dev shrugged. "We-ell?" he asked leadingly.

"I'll do it," I said decisively. "I'll do it."

"Yee-haw!" Dev let out a bloodcurdling Rebel yell.

"Shhh!" the WoW nerds exploded. Dev shot them his fiercest glare.

"But, um, a question," I asked. "Why are we Confederates? We're from Minnesota. That's about as north as you can get. Not only geographically, but also historically Northern. As in fought for the Union. Minnesota became a state right before the war, in 1858, and sent troops to Bull Run, Gettysburg, Antietam . . . all the major battles. Besides, the South *lost.* Why would we want to be on the losing side? And we haven't even addressed the fact that their ideology was inherently corrupt!"

"Duh, better outfits," he countered. "Yankee girls were plain, plain, *plain!* I want *giant* hoop skirts and ribbons and lace! And statistically, for whatever reason, Confederate reenactors spend more on their gear. Plus there are more of them. All that 'Lost Cause' business really makes you shell out, apparently. Buy back the glory of Dixie!"

"Okay. But not to sound racist," I started hesitantly.

"Libs, we're talking Confederacy. A little bit racist is kind of a given."

"Okay, okay," I agreed. "Will it be awkward to be a Confederate and, um—"

"Sexy like milk chocolate?" he interrupted.

"I was gonna go with 'not white.'"

"Sexy like a Twix bar?"

"Or 'Indian.'"

"Sexy like a Kit Kat bar? Break me off a piece of that! Ow!" he yelped, as I smacked his arm.

"Yes, yes, sexy like any number of milk chocolate–flavored confections," I said, attempting to stop him before he could go through the entire contents of the vending machine.

"Clark Gable was, like, super tan. I'm not worried. Margaret Mitchell herself wrote that Rhett Butler was, quote, 'swarthy as a pirate,' unquote, and who is more pirate swarthy than me?" he finished.

"Wow, you actually researched something. I'm impressed.

And, quite frankly, astonished." I decided not to harp on the fact that *Gone with the Wind* was not exactly the epitome of historical accuracy, presenting, as it did, the mid-nineteenth century through a twentieth-century Technicolor lens.

"There are greenbacks to be made, Miss Libby. We go to the South to worship at the altar of King Cotton! And King Taffeta! And King Silk Moiré!"

"So basically you want to be carpetbaggers."

"Not just any carpetbaggers," he corrected me. "We are Prada carpetbaggers. And don't you forget it."

I didn't forget. And almost before I knew it, senior year had fled by, my faux Prada carpetbags were packed, and I was at the last event of high school, before heading off to the Civil War and then on to college.

"So this is prom." Garrett looked around, taking in the foil stars hanging from the ceiling and the crinkly crepe paper bedecking the walls. "I thought I'd escaped it, but it got me in the end."

"You mean you're not feeling the 'Enchantment Under the Stars'?" I asked, poking him in the ribs as I quoted our prom theme.

"I wouldn't say that." He smiled. "The stars may leave a little something to be desired, but 'enchanting' doesn't even begin to describe the way you look tonight."

I blushed, turning a darker shade than the pale pink prom dress Dev had made for me. It felt almost like Garrett and I were the only two people in the world, or at the least all alone in our own magical corner of the St. Paul Crowne Plaza Hotel

Event Room. In actuality, we were just one small island in a sea of partying St. Paul Academy Pioneers. And we were sharing our island with Dev and his date, whose name I couldn't pronounce to save my life, as well as two of my fellow sopranos from chorus, plus their dates. My chorus friends were busy trying to harmonize to "Firework," with moderately successful results, as their dates were heavily invested in a game of paper football featuring a cocktail napkin in the pivotal role.

"Explain to me how you made it to your advanced age without experiencing *the* quintessential high school experience," Dev asked from across the table, as he poked his rubbery piece of chicken.

"Why doesn't someone explain to *me* why they bother with plated dinner service at this bourgeois fest of mundaniness? Or how they have the audacity to pass off this reconstituted meat byproduct as dinner?" Dev's date complained loudly.

"Why doesn't someone explain to *him* that 'mundaniness' is not a word?" Garrett whispered.

Stifling a laugh, I choked on my Diet Coke, giving the chicken a wayward glance. "It is pretty bad," I agreed. "Fee—Fy—Uh, how do you pronounce your name again?"

"It's Fyodr," he drawled. "And this is inedible."

"He's vegan," Dev whispered proudly. "Garrett? Advanced age? Paucity of social experience?"

"I think the real mystery is why anyone would *want* to go to prom," Garrett grumbled good-naturedly. "But before now, there wasn't anyone worth enduring this for."

"Whatever Libby wants," Dev sang off-key, "Libby gets."

"Oh, come on!" I lobbed a piece of dinner roll across the

table. It bounced off Dev's nose, and he stopped butchering *Damn Yankees.* "It's not like I *forced* him. I didn't force you, right?"

"Of course not." Garrett chuckled as he poked at a limp green bean. "You're five foot three. I don't think you could force anyone to do anything."

"Don't make me use this." I brandished my remaining dinner roll at him.

"Seriously, Libby, of course you didn't force me. I wanted to come. Because even if I don't completely understand why it's important to you, it is. So it's important to me."

"Adorable," Dev said drily. "Fyodr, why don't you regale us all with your eyebrow-grooming regime again."

"Come on, you must get it at least a little. Why it's important, I mean," I clarified for Garrett. "It's such an iconic cultural touchstone! Didn't you ever watch *Pretty in Pink*? *Never Been Kissed*? *Footloose*? *She's All That*?"

"You never wanted your very own Laney Boggs moment?" Dev asked.

"Is that a disease?" Garrett asked.

"Ignore him. And, you, focus on your vegan," I reprimanded Dev.

"Regardless, none of those movies make me want to go to prom. They just make me break out in a cold sweat at the thought of all that dancing."

"Har-har." I crumbled my remaining dinner roll in my mouth and chewed its cottony substance.

"And now that we've completed this journey through cinematic prom classics, Libby," Garrett said, as he pushed out his chair and stood up from the table, pulling up to his full height, a dangling silver star threatening to tangle itself in his messy brown hair, "may I have this dance? As long as you don't mind the cold sweat."

"Bring it on," I said, smiling as I stood.

"Just try not to trip on the dress!" Dev called, as we crossed to the dance floor. "That's dupioni silk!"

I rolled my eyes as Garrett pulled me close to him.

"I'll try not to wrinkle you, I promise."

"A little bit of wrinkling never hurt anyone," I said, as I leaned my head against his chest, still a head shorter than him even in my heels.

In a stroke of good fortune or careful planning on Garrett's part, the DJ switched to a slow song, so all he had to do was sway. I mean, really, he was lucky this wasn't a hundred years ago, because then he'd have had to waltz. I chuckled a little, imagining the panic that would seize Garrett if the DJ unexpectedly segued into "The Blue Danube."

"What's so funny?" Garrett murmured into my ear.

"You waltzing," I replied.

"Hey, now," he said, mock offended. "I think I'm acquitting myself pretty well with this shuffling technique."

"Absolutely," I agreed. "And you look very handsome in your tux." He really did, too. He looked like a tall, lanky, not particularly lethal spy. "Actually, you look a little bit like—"

"James Bond's IT guy?" he interrupted.

"More like the guy Flynn Rider plays in that TV show."

"First of all, Libby, Flynn Rider is not a real person."

"But—"

"Cartoon, Libby. He's a cartoon." He held up his arm and motioned me under it. "Second, I believe you are referring to the actor Zachary Levi, who plays special agent Charles 'Chuck' Bartowski in the eponymous television show."

"Did you just *spin* me?" I asked with disbelief, as I completed my turn.

"Watch out, McCaffrey's gettin' fancy." He next did something that could only be described as a jazz hand.

"You're actually enjoying this, aren't you?" Garrett. Enjoying dancing. Now that was something I never thought I'd see.

"Libby, I have fun with you no matter what we do. Because I'm with you."

And even though I knew I was setting myself up for a stern lecture on appropriate prom behavior from Ms. Heitkamp, I grabbed his lapels and kissed him.

But before Heitkamp could barrel down on us, we were startled apart by Ke$ha blaring out of the speakers at the approximate decibel of a jet engine. A flicker of pure pain crossed Garrett's face.

"Wanna go outside?" I offered.

"You are the *best* girlfriend," he exclaimed, crushing me to his chest in an enthusiastic hug. "Come on, Tiny, let's blow this Popsicle stand."

"Tiny?" I laughed as he grabbed my hand and led me off the dance floor. "You're in a particularly heightist mood today."

"Just testing it out. Thought you might need a nickname. Something to put on the back of your Amherst jersey."

"I don't know what sport you think I'll be playing at Amherst—"

"Rounders? Croquet? Fencing?" He shrugged. "I didn't think I'd play a sport in college, but now I'm one of the finest keepers that Tufts Quidditch has to offer."

"Garrett, your commitment to the nerdification of America is truly impressive."

"Careful in that glass house, closet nerd." His eyes twinkled as he pushed open the double doors to the patio space.

The patio was mostly empty, except for a few of the guys from my AP English class choreographing a lightsaber battle in a dark corner. I sent up a silent prayer that Garrett wouldn't be tempted to join them. Fortunately, we blew right past *Revenge of the Sith* and made for the stone wall demarcating the end of the patio. It was low enough that even I could hop up and sit on it without any problems.

"Are you sad?" he asked softly.

"About what? High school being over?"

He nodded.

"Not particularly." I shrugged. "I'll miss seeing Dev every day, of course, and my parents, but mostly I just feel excited to start college. And to be in the same state as you."

"A marked improvement," he said with a grin. "How ever will you while away the tedious hours between now and autumn?"

"Life with Dev is never dull. And if they intend to cram four years of Civil War into one summer, things must be pretty fast-paced."

"You sure there's no Yankee reenactment on Boston Common you can do instead?" he asked, holding my hand.

"Pretty sure," I said reluctantly. "But the summer will fly by.

You'll be super busy at the newspaper, and I'll be busy—"

"Staving off dysentery?" he supplied helpfully.

"And before we know it," I continued, "we'll be together."

"Summer in Dixie, fall in Boston."

"Exactly." I grinned. "Trust me. The time will fly."

chapter one

"Wait, listen! Listen. In Virginia in 1864, at a dance that the Union soldiers held, some of the soldiers dressed up as women because not enough local women would attend: 'Some of the real women went, but the boy girls were so much better looking that they left. . . . Some of them looked almost good enough to lay with and I guess some of them did get laid with.'" Dev looked up from his copy of *The Story the Soldiers Wouldn't Tell: Sex in the Civil War* and grinned. "You hear that? They got laid with!"

"Of course I can hear you—you're two inches away from my face and shouting."

We were on a teeny-tiny plane we'd boarded in Charlotte, North Carolina—or what our very friendly pilot had informed us was a "puddah jumpah." After about fifteen seconds, I deciphered his accent and figured out he'd said "puddle jumper"—which was a pretty accurate description. I swore I could hear the wind whistling through cracks in the siding. We were snuggled in so tight, I was practically sitting on Dev's lap, and his Fred Perry track-jacketed elbow was perilously close to knocking into the little old lady across the aisle.

"Chapter Eleven is just full of interesting nuggets." Dev flipped a page. "Even Walt Whitman had an easy time picking up dudes. And look!" Dev held up the book, open to a black-

and-white photograph of an old guy with a bushy white beard. "Whitman was one ugly 'mo. I am way cuter. If he can meet guys in the 1860s, so can I."

The old lady across from us, who had already been eyeing Dev's book cover suspiciously, reached up to pat her immobile steel-gray curls nervously.

"Dev," I hissed over the roar of the engine, "while I am beyond pleased that you're taking an interest in history, maybe a little quieter—"

"Lincoln!" he shouted triumphantly. "Looks like that tall drink of water preferred to spend his nights with unmarried men, according to one Dr. Thomas P. Lowry!"

Alarmed, the woman across the aisle reached into the floral-patterned bag that matched her pantsuit to pull out a Bible. I flipped my *Martha Stewart Living* closed, in case this escalated to an attempted exorcism and I needed both hands free to prevent a certain eavesdropping old lady from trying to get the devil out of Dev.

"Oooh!" Dev squealed. "He had a little boy toy named Joshua Speed; they lived together and slept in the same bed, mind you, while they were young lawyers, like *Law and Order: Gay Intent* or *Illinois Legal* or *Ally McQueer,* and—"

"Dev." I nudged him and subtly nodded toward our eavesdropper.

We turned slightly, peering across the aisle. Dev was wearing an "I'd Hit That" T-shirt with a picture of a piñata on it; the T-shirt was so tight you could see his nipples through it. The lady with the Bible was staring at the fuzzy-flocked letters on his chest like she was trying to crack the Da Vinci Code.

"Dorothy"—he raised his book to cover our faces so we

could whisper behind it—"I have a feeling we're not in St. Paul anymore."

"Flight attendants, please prepare for landing," a voice drawled over the speakers with an accent so thick you could have swirled a spoon through it. "Ladies and gents, please return your seats and tray tables to their upright positions, and turn off all approved electronic devices."

The engine roared louder and louder as we made our descent. I smooshed my face against the glass, and Dev leaned over me to look too, as we took in our first view of Montgomery.

"'Sweet home Alabama,'" Dev sang into my ear as we drew closer and closer to the spread of green trees and sprawl of buildings.

We hit the ground and bumped along the runway.

"'Where the skies are so blue'" Dev sang as the rest of the plane applauded the pilot's safe landing.

The woman across the aisle crossed herself.

Dev played a few licks on his air guitar as the captain turned off the FASTEN SEAT BELT sign. Dev continued to sing quietly as we collected our carry-ons and shuffled into the aisle. The old lady, still clutching her Bible, deliberately avoided eye contact.

When we finally exited the plane, we stepped into an oven.

"Holy crap, it's hot!" I shrieked as we walked down the portable stairs onto the runway.

"Oh, come on, it's not that bad." Dev pulled on his sunglasses and smiled into the sunshine.

"Yes, it is!" I cried. It was like trying to walk through solid air. I didn't know heat like this existed. I could feel sunburn forming on every inch of my exposed midwestern pallor.

"Please," he scoffed. "This isn't hot. You've never been to

Aunt Lakshmi's birthday party in Mumbai in August."

"Obviously not!" I retorted. "The Keltings are like sixth-generation Minnesotans. We are winter people. The frosty blood of the Norse flows in my veins! Give me four feet of snow over this inferno any day!"

"Oookay, drama Viking." Dev rolled his eyes. "Move your little Nordic butt. We have a lot of luggage to get."

"Seriously, Dev." I followed him off the tarmac into Montgomery Regional Airport and the sweet relief of blessed air conditioning. "Why Alabama?"

"Oh, come now, Libby, you know why," Dev replied breezily.

"Because the Confederate States of America were formed in Montgomery in February 1861? Because it served as the first capital of the CSA? Because it was the inauguration site of Jefferson Davis, the first and only Confederate president? Because the order to fire on Fort Sumter, the act that started the entire war, was sent from here?" I rattled off every historical reason I could think of.

"No." Dev shook his head. "Because no other southern state boasts its very own Reese Witherspoon rom-com. Obvi."

"Seriously." I followed him toward the baggage claim, winding our way through airport halls that had white Corinthian columns in them, like a plantation porch. "We're spending the summer in Hades because of *Sweet Home Alabama*?"

"But of course," he said, as we parked ourselves in front of the baggage claim. "All signs pointed to Alabama. Reese Witherspoon *played* a fashion designer—hello! It was like a cosmic sign! Plus that movie is bursting with cute guys. And there's even a gay one," he finished triumphantly. "What other southern state has all that?"

"Sweet Jesus," I muttered. My bag vibrated against my hip. "Service!" I shouted gleefully. "It's back!"

Dev gave me one of his looks as the baggage claim started up a slow *chug-chug* and began spitting out luggage, one piece at a time. I dug around for my phone and hastily flipped it open.

There was a text from Garrett waiting in my in box:

> HOPE YOU MADE IT SAFELY SOUTH TO THE RED STATES — IS IT TOO LATE TO GO BLUE? OR ARE YOU ALREADY WHISTLING DIXIE?

I grinned. Despite my many lengthy treatises on the differences in Southern and Northern nineteenth-century fashion, Garrett could not understand why on earth we didn't want to be Yankees. Or why we wanted to spend the summer in a state that hadn't been carried by a Democratic presidential candidate since 1976.

"You know I'm a Yankee at heart. I'm just a pushover for a hoop skirt," I texted back. Which was true. I mean, obviously I understood all of Garrett's many arguments on the ethical ramifications of participating in the glorification of a society that condoned the ownership of human beings, but Dev reminded me that a passion for fashion was a higher calling. One above silly things like politics or morality. "How's your first day at the Daily Planet, Clark Kent?" I added.

Garrett wasn't actually working for the *Daily Planet,* of course, that being the fictional newspaper that employed Superman. He was so excited about interning at the *Boston Globe* this summer, he'd created a countdown calendar to his first day of work. Which would have been lame if it wasn't so cute.

"Okay," he texted back. "I have to go. I'll call you later."

Okay? Just okay? Huh. That was certainly not the glowingly enthusiastic response I'd been expecting.

"A little help here, Textarella?" Dev grunted, heaving an enormous bag off the conveyor belt. We had just barely squeaked under the baggage weight restriction, as each of our suitcases was stuffed to the gills with "Confederate Couture." Dev assured me that we had enough outfits to last the two of us all summer, but he wouldn't hesitate to sell the clothes off my back if a prospective customer was interested. As for the rest of the fashions, earlier in the week I'd helped him lug a few enormous boxes down to FedEx, where we shipped them off to a mysterious address in Pine Level, Alabama. I dropped my phone back in my bag, shrugging off Garrett's less-than-thrilled response, and ambled over to help Dev. He'd already muscled my pink behemoth of a suitcase off the conveyor belt, but luckily his zebra-striped monster wasn't too far behind. Together, struggling, we pulled it to the floor.

"Jesus," I said, wiping some sweat off my forehead. "If all those Southern belles had carried their wardrobes everywhere, they would have been ripped."

"I know, right?" Dev extended the handle on his suitcase, ready to wheel it away. "We should have started lifting last semester. Good thing we're in the land of chivalry, and hopefully you can just bat those baby blues and get some good ol' boy to heave 'em around from now on."

"That sounds like a much better plan," I agreed, as Dev started to head toward the exit. I wheeled my suitcase behind him. "Um, where are we going?" I had just realized a fatal flaw in Dev's plan. "How are we getting all the way out to the camp? Taxi? We can't rent a car or anything; we're too young . . ."

Our first event was an instruction camp at Confederate Memorial Park, which was a ways outside the city. If Garrett knew I was spending the night at a place called the Confederate Memorial Park, or that one even existed, he probably would have popped a gasket.

"Not to worry, it is all taken care of." Dev lowered his sunglasses and strode confidently into the sunshine. I followed and wilted immediately. This heat would be the death of me. My obituary would be something tragically embarrassing like "Teen Girl Dies; Too Pale to Function. 'I Knew She Should Have Been a Yankee,' Boyfriend Says Sadly." Maybe they'd arrest Dev for being my de facto murderer, and at least my spirit would be avenged.

A bright teal minivan pulled up to the curb and parked directly in front of us. I shot Dev a quizzical look.

"I knew that big ol' suitcase had to be you!" Paula Deen's doppelgänger was barreling out of the driver's seat toward us. "Who else in the Montgomery Regional Airport would have a zebra-striped suitcase, I swear! You are somethin' else, dumplin'." She pulled him close to her magenta-colored bosom, enveloping him in a giant hug. Someone wearing more pink than I was? I was starting to like Alabama already.

"Mrs. Anderson, I presume?" Dev asked once he'd extricated himself.

"Please, I'm Tammy, hon. And this must be Libby!" She hugged me tightly, before holding me at arm's length. "Now, let me get a good look at you. My goodness, you're even prettier than Dev said you were!"

Dev smirked. I blushed.

"Did he not tell you I was comin', darlin'?" Tammy asked me. "You look plumb rattled. Oh, land sakes." She rolled her eyes fondly at Dev, who shrugged good-naturedly in a "Who, me?" kind of way. "I'm Tammy Anderson, civilian coordinator of the Fifteenth Alabama Volunteer Infantry." Her chest puffed up with pride. "Welcome to 'Bama!"

"Thanks." I smiled.

"Now, why go on an' keep her in the dark?" She swatted Dev's arm playfully. "Men, huh?" She turned to me for sympathy. "Good for nothin' but openin' pickle jars and liftin' heavy things," she said. "Speakin' of . . ." She eyed our bags. "I'll be right back. Don't y'all dare lift a finger. Ladies don't need to lift nothin'."

She left, presumably in search of a gallant young man.

"Isn't she fantastic?" Dev gushed.

Tammy returned not a moment later, gallant young man in tow. He easily loaded our suitcases into the back of the minivan, before touching his hand to the brim of his Auburn Tigers cap and telling us to have a nice day.

Dev raised an eyebrow. "I could get used to this southern charm thing," he whispered. "See? I knew Reese Witherspoon wouldn't steer us wrong. It's like a recipe for a rom-com down here with all these scruffy square jaws."

"Now, y'all gonna keep flappin' your gums, or y'all gonna get in the van?" Tammy called, waiting in the driver's seat.

"SHOTGUN!" Dev screamed, and rocketed into the front seat.

I rolled my eyes and clambered in back.

"Sir, you are no gentleman," Tammy admonished him.

"And you, miss, are no lady," he replied.

"Don't I know it!" She laughed and drove out of the airport.

Granted, we were driving away from the city, but the minute we left the airport, things got real rural, real fast. We passed fields with weather-beaten split-rail fences and big old trees, horses grazing in knee-high grass, and, yes, a pickup truck rusting by the side of the road. There was no question about it—I was south of the Mason-Dixon Line.

"It's so nice to finally meet you," Dev said, as he checked his reflection in the mirror by the sun flap, fixing his hair so it spiked up jauntily.

"I know, darlin', I know." Tammy patted his knee with her non-driving hand. "We are so lucky to have snapped you up! Most sutlers don't agree to spend the whole summer with the reenactors, livin' in the tents and all like they do, but I swear it will triple your profits. Authenticity is the name of the game," she said wisely, "and nothin' says authentic like a belly full of hardtack and a tent full of mosquitoes."

I shot Dev a worried look. I mean, I love authenticity too, but I'm not exactly used to . . . roughing it. And Dev had the highest thread-count sheets of anyone I knew. Seriously. As I learned from an old episode of MTV *Cribs,* they were the same as Kanye West's.

"That's me," Dev said, "authentic all the way." I could practically hear the dollar signs going off in his head as he chanted quietly, "Triple the profits."

"And talented!" Tammy added. "Have you seen this boy's work?"

I nodded.

"I swear, the minute he e-mailed me the pictures of his

dresses, I went straight to the captain and said we have *got* to snap this boy up!" She snapped for emphasis. "I watch that *Project Runway;* I know a top designer when I see one."

Dev preened.

"And, you"—she kept right on going, looking at me in her rearview mirror—"just as pretty as any of them models! Beau's sure gonna be sorry he couldn't come and pick y'all up at the airport."

"Beau . . . ?" Dev asked, one eyebrow raised, a sure sign that his interest had been piqued.

"Beauregard. Beau, for short. My son." She rifled around in her purse—her one-handed driving skills were truly impressive—and handed Dev a small snapshot. "He'll be drivin' you from battle to battle, totin' all your stuff in the back of his truck, but he had to get the camp all sorted out this morning."

"Has it started already? Did we miss anything?" I asked anxiously.

"Nothin', nothin' at all, darlin', don't you fret," Tammy reassured me. "This was for officers only."

"Quite a good-looking boy, Tammy!" Dev appraised the photo, clearly approving of what he saw, which must have meant that Beau was cute, because Dev was nothing if not picky. He showed it to me, but I was too far back to get anything but a glimpse of a cute auburn-haired blur in a football uniform.

"Well, I sure think so, but I'm biased. And he just got promoted!" Tammy said proudly. "That's why he wasn't here. Youngest officer in the Fifteenth—in Fifteenth history, as a matter of fact! Well, except for during the actual . . . unpleasantness," she said, swallowing. "But the youngest in the history of the Fifteenth Volunteer Infantry. Course, he'd shrug it off and say he's the lowest-rankin' officer there, and nothin' but an NCO."

"'NCO'?" I asked.

"A non-commissioned officer," she explained.

"I don't even know what a regular commissioned officer is," Dev piped up.

"Well, in the real army, commissioned officers, like generals and things, were trained at West Point, or other military schools, and given authority from the government," Tammy explained. "They get their command straight from the top. It's a little bit different in a reenactment. You work your way up from the ranks, and when the present captain retires, the first lieutenant is promoted. And the first lieutenant's appointed by the captain, so he picks his successor. And so on and so on, down the line."

"And NCO?" I asked again.

"An NCO is an enlisted member of the armed forces who's given command by a commissioned officer, not by the government itself. In military reenactments, they're elected by the other soldiers in the company. That's how corporals and sergeants get chosen in the Fifteenth Alabama. Ain't as prestigious maybe, but I think it's wonderful to know that the men you're fightin' with have faith in you. Trust you. Respect you. To be chosen by your peers, you know?" She smiled. "I'm awful proud."

"So kind of like a People's Choice Award instead of an Oscar?" Dev mused as he gently placed the photograph back in her cavernous purse.

"Sure, darlin', whatever floats your boat," Tammy replied

evenly. She took a particularly sharp turn, and the silver angel charm hanging from the rearview mirror swung wide and hit Dev smack in the forehead.

"Oooh, sorry, darlin'!" she called.

"No worries." Dev picked it up and read off the charm above the angel, "'Never Drive Faster Than Your Guardian Angel Can Fly.'"

"Cute, huh?" Tammy grinned. "I keep trying to get Beau to put one up—the way that boy drives, he needs it." She chuckled fondly. "'Specially in that rusty old heap of his. 'Beau,' I said to him, I said, 'Beau, I don't care what your name is, you ain't on the *Dukes of Hazzard,* and that old truck ain't no General Lee,' and he said, 'Mama, I have no idea what you're on about—I don't watch movies with Jessica Simpson in them.' Jessica Simpson!" She laughed. "Don't that boy just beat all?"

"I'd let him beat my—"

"So where are we going?" I interjected. "Up to the battlefield? To the park?"

"Park's up in Marbury," Tammy answered, "and we're headed that way. Not too far off now. But first, we're stoppin' off at my place. It's in Pine Level, right on the way. Because we sure can't have y'all showin' up lookin' like that!" she said, laughing.

Ouch. I looked down. Okay, maybe I was a little bedraggled after all our flight time, but my baby blue lounge pants weren't exactly schlubby sweats—they had a pin-tucked front and ballet pink ribbon drawstring, and the color scheme was echoed in my vintage print Alice in Wonderland tee, for Pete's sake!

"She means we need to wear period costumes," Dev drawled. "I saw where your mind went."

"Oh, no, honey, you look fine," Tammy assured me as we

drove past a sign proudly proclaiming PINE LEVEL: THE BEST LITTLE PLACE TO LIVE!

Dev snorted.

"It's just that those old goats will crucify you if you show up in any kind of pants. Or anything that came into vogue any later than 1864," she said with a smirk. "And you can't come back from that. First impressions are everything with these old judgie-wudgies."

"I always make an impression," Dev said grandly.

"Honey, of that I have no doubt." Tammy turned down a driveway, passing a swinging white sign that read SWEET HOME-AWAY-FROM-HOME ALABAMA BED AND BREAKFAST.

Around the corner, a gorgeous pale pink Victorian complete with wraparound porch, turrets, and gingerbread on the eaves materialized out of the trees. We pulled up right in front, under another SWEET HOME-AWAY-FROM-HOME ALABAMA sign hanging over the front porch.

"Oh, how beautiful." I sighed. "It looks just like my old dollhouse!"

"That's exactly what I was goin' for." Tammy turned off the car. "Welcome to Pine Level's best B&B!"

"Dev, which suitcase should we open?" I asked as we all climbed out of the minivan.

"None." He patted his carry-on with assurance. "I planned ahead. Everything we need is in here."

"Come on in, y'all, come in!" Tammy called from the porch. We scampered after her.

Inside it was just as cute—a vision in soft butter walls and rose-printed curtains. We stood facing a little check-in desk that opened onto a parlor with overstuffed couches and stacks of board games on a mahogany coffee table. Another door, cracked open, led to a formal dining room.

"Southern chic!" Dev approved. "Love it."

"Now, the house has been in the family since it was built in the 1880s, but it was me and Mr. Anderson—God rest his soul—who converted it into a B&B. Not too long before Beau was born, matter of fact," Tammy explained, as she led us up the stairs. "Not too many guests here right now. Any, actually. Gets quiet in the summer. Not surprising." She chuckled ruefully. "Most folks aren't brave enough to face 'Bama in this heat!"

"I fear nothing," Dev proclaimed.

I feared heat stroke just a little bit. But I decided to keep that to myself.

"Fearless. Just like me." She smiled. "I knew we were gonna get on great. A boy after my own heart. Now," she said, stopping at the top of the stairs, poised before the threshold of a door bearing a hand-painted sign with a picture of a big pink flower on it. "This here's the Camellia Room." She indicated the door. "State flower of Alabama!" she added proudly. "Y'all can change in there. There's a screen, honey, so you can have some privacy." She smiled at me. "Now, most importantly, y'all ever had sweet tea? Real sweet tea?"

We shook our heads.

"Oh, y'all are in for a treat!" She clapped her hands. "I'll fix us some while y'all freshen up. Come on down to the parlor when y'all are set."

Tammy headed down the stairs, and I pushed open the door to the Camellia Room. It must have been the room inside the turret, because the pale pink walls curved around us. Lace curtains fluttered at the window and hung down from the canopy bed. I flung myself onto it.

"I think this is what heaven looks like," I said, sighing.

"Libby Kelting heaven, maybe," Dev replied. "I think heaven is a flock of male models skinny-dipping in a sea of iced coffee."

"Let's just stay here forever," I said, stretching out. "This bed is really comfy. And everything's so pink. This would be much better than a tent. Let's just stay."

"Can't do that." Dev set his carry-on bag down next to a white wooden end table bearing a porcelain pitcher decorated with painted camellias. "Eyes on the prize, Libby."

"And what is the prize again? Because this bed deserves a prize."

"Gucci, Pucci, Dior, and more," he recited as he started unpacking, laying out items of clothing over the back of the camellia-covered armchair by the window. "Just keep repeating that to yourself. That's what I do. I'm making enough money so I can start college looking like I spent the summer in effin' Milan ripping clothes off the backs of runway models. And that makes all the tents, cots, and mosquitoes in the world worth it. You can spend your share on whatever you want. Even on a . . . I don't know . . ." He cast around for an idea. "A spinning wheel."

"A spinning wheel?" I propped myself up on my elbows to shoot him an incredulous look.

"I don't know what you history types go for!" He shrugged. "It just popped into my head."

"Well, I could get a really nice stand mixer," I thought suddenly. "I've never had one, and Martha Stewart uses one for *everything,* so it could really take my pastry up a notch—"

"I liked you better lying down than discussing kitchen appliances," he interrupted. I frowned at him and plopped back down on the bed. Ah, bliss. "Take a nap while I change, Sleeping Beauty, and then I'll help you get dressed."

"Mmm," I agreed, eyes already falling closed.

Far too soon, Dev shook me awake. He was in his shirtsleeves, wearing a herringbone vest over a snowy cotton shirt, a casually tied silk cravat, and pants tucked into boots that reminded me of my time horseback riding at Girl Scout Camp Shingobee Timbers in the Chippewa National Forest. I saw a navy blue frock coat draped over the camellia chair, waiting for him.

"Come on, lazy," he reprimanded, as he shook me again. "Time to get dressed."

Groggily, I sat up. "What time is it?" I wondered. "Is it tomorrow?"

"It's twelve minutes later." He rolled his eyes. "Stand." I did. "Here," he said, handing me a pile of white things. "Put these on, and then I'll corset you. Go on, behind the screen." He shooed me away. "Better start getting into character now. Modesty and all that."

Obediently, I marched behind the curved wooden panels of the white Victorian dressing screen. Okay, things were looking good. I pulled on a white cotton off-the-shoulder chemise and a pair of lace-trimmed pantaloons. I was impressed with Dev's historical accuracy. He'd chosen not to sew the crotch seam, but to use a ribbon to tie the pantaloons together in back, like they would have done in the 1860s so ladies could relieve themselves more easily. I decided to keep my polka dot underwear on. It felt a little too drafty, otherwise. And then . . .

"Stockings?! No. Not cool. In this heat? You've got to be kidding me."

"Not kidding. I'm wearing pants, princess. Pull 'em on," Dev ordered. "And they're cotton, anyway. It won't be that bad. 'Bama belles wore cotton stockings all summer long in the 1860s. You can do it too."

I picked up the two elastic garters that had fallen out of the pile and secured the stockings above my knees. Now dressed head to toe in white, I skipped out from behind the screen.

"'Here comes Suzy Snowflake, dressed in a snow-white gown,'" I sang merrily.

"What the eff are you singing?" Dev asked.

"It was my solo at the Eunice Norton Elementary Holiday Concert in fifth grade . . . never mind . . ." I said, trailing off. I blushed.

"I'm never sure if I love you in spite of the fact that you're so effin' weird, or because of it," he said fondly. "And now"—he held up a strapless white cotton twill corset—"it's go time."

The corset was not nearly as soft as my other cotton underthings, with its steel boning to mold my waist into the appropriate hourglass shape. A series of brass grommets marched up the front to where the corset ended, just high enough to not be considered indecent exposure but low enough that I couldn't wear it in public without blushing. Standing behind me, Dev was gaily tugging away at the strings that were lacing up my back over my chemise.

"Tight enough, don't you think?" I gasped.

"Not by a long shot," he grunted. "Hold that pole."

Just like Scarlett O'Hara, I took ahold of the canopy's bedpost, pulling my shoulder blades together to get the proper silhouette. Wow, that was tight. The corset dug into my ribs, causing my breath to come in quick, shallow gasps. Last summer, when I'd worn eighteenth-century stays, they weren't nearly this tight. Back in the 1700s, the main function of stays was to provide support. But by the 1840s and '50s, after stays had transformed into corsets, "tightlacing" became popular—that is, lacing the corset so tightly in order to have the smallest waist possible. In the 1860s, waist minimization was the name of the game—a game I currently felt I was losing.

"Miss Libby, you keep eatin' them French fries, you ain't never gonna have no eighteen-inch waist again," Dev barked.

"I never had an eighteen-inch waist to begin with! I'm not a mutant freak!" I protested. "And French fries are delicious."

"One more big pull," he said. "There!" He tied the laces in a knot, panting. "Perfect."

Slightly dizzy, I let Dev lead me over to the full-length mirror. I'll give the corset this much—it worked. My waist looked infinitesimally tiny. Especially in comparison to the enormity of my cleavage.

"There are my moneymakers," he said, patting the tops of my boobs proprietarily.

"Oh, stop it." I swatted him away. "They wouldn't be so . . . out there if you didn't lace it so tightly."

"That's the whole point, darling." He rolled his eyes. "I'm gonna use what your mama gave you. Buy Confederate Couture, and you, too, can be this ta-ta-licious!"

"That better not be your slogan," I warned.

"I already put it on a promotional coffee mug," he deadpanned, and reached for a four-tiered hoop skirt covered in white cotton that had been waiting at the foot of the bed.

"How the hell did you fit that into your carry-on?" I asked, mystified. Sure, Dev's carry-on was so big he could barely wedge it into the overhead compartment, but this seemed contrary to the laws of physics.

"Just call me Gary Poppins." He held out the hoop as I stepped into it. "I have a magical carpetbag."

"Seriously." I shot him a look as he tied the hoop around my waist.

"It's collapsible," he admitted giddily. "Plastic, collapsible hoop skirts were popular in the fifties for wearing under full dresses to give you that perfect Betty Draper look. Très *Mad Men*. I modified that idea to work with yours. Travel hoops! I think they could be *very* hot this year."

I stood speechless as he helped me pull a very full petticoat with three ruffles over the top of the whole operation. I mean, I had always known Dev was smart, but this was just pure genius.

"No more underwear, right?" I asked as I emerged from under the petticoat. I knew that real Southern belles had worn as many as five petticoats, and even though they wore fewer petticoats in the summer, I was half-afraid Dev thought one wouldn't cut it. Despite the fact that heat stroke was a distinct possibility.

"No, no, dress time." He held up a soft Wedgwood blue bundle dotted with bouquets of cerulean-blue and snow-white flowers. I help up my arms, and Dev pulled it over my head. The skirt cascaded over the hoop in five flounces, separated from the bodice by a cerulean-blue silk sash. The bodice was off the shoulder, with cerulean-blue bows at the sleeves and the V-neck. Both the sleeves and the neckline were framed with pleated froths of white lace. It was stunning.

"You like?" he asked. "The fabric print is called 'Maiden's Bouquet,' and the dress is called the 'Juliet.' I took it from a *Godey's Lady's Book* printed in 1860. What is that magazine, like, the Civil War *Cosmo*?"

"Imagine if *Better Homes and Gardens* and *Vogue* had a baby. In the nineteenth century," I decided, admiring myself in the mirror. Goodness, my waist looked tiny. I felt like I was floating above the graceful swell of my skirt.

"It's not bad. It could use more quizzes . . ." He drifted off for a minute. "But, anyway," he said, coming back to the present. "They took it from a Chestnut Street dressmaker in Philadelphia, and I took it from them. For you."

"It's amazing," I gushed. "Only . . ." I worried for a moment, thinking about what Tammy had said, about judgie-wudgie reenactors. "It's not too much?" I asked anxiously. "Too Twelve Oaks barbecue? When Mammy didn't want Scarlett to wear a dress that was too low-cut?"

"I say you can show your bosoms whenever you want," he replied stubbornly. "And it's way after three o'clock."

"True fact." I winked at my reflection. I was feeling sassier already—maybe I was a natural at this Southern belle stuff.

"And it's all about first impressions," Dev continued, as he crossed over to the dressing table to fix his hair in the mirror. He picked up a silver-backed brush and started smoothing it into a side part, as opposed to his usually spiky 'do. "This is the first taste the world will get of Confederate Couture. We need to go in there with a bang. You know me—it's 'Go big or go home.' And thanks to your corset cleavage, we're going big."

"Hey!" I protested.

"Good first impressions, Libby. Speaking of which. . ." He eyed me critically, hairbrush in hand. "We need to do something about that."

"I can't help it," I moaned, as Dev poked the helmet of frizz on my head. "It's the humidity. Please tell me you have bobby pins."

"Please." He rolled his eyes as he emptied his pockets, displaying bobby pins, safety pins, a tiny sewing kit, some ribbon, and what looked like a handful of smooshed Jujubes. "Who do you think you're dealing with?"

I eagerly snatched up the bobby pins and started to wrangle my hair into manageable curls, with the front pieces held back with jaunty little blue bows. Thanks to an epically humid Kelting family vacation to Fort Lauderdale a few years ago, I'd learned the best way to tame the beast.

"It's a little more of a 1930s conception of the 1860s than actually 1860s," Dev commented, wincing once I'd finished. He was right—it was not totally dissimilar to Vivien Leigh's hair for most of *Gone with the Wind.* "But I think you did the best you could, given the circumstances. Attempting anything more elaborate might have angered the curl monsters."

"It is *humid.*" I swatted him playfully. "And it's not monstrous—it's . . . um . . . voluminous."

"Just keep telling yourself that." He held out his elbow. "Shall we? I hear talk of sweet tea in the parlor," he drawled.

"Land sakes," I said, as I took his arm, "do go on."

We navigated our way out of the Camellia Room, Dev stopping to pick up his carpetbag as I turned sideways and tilted my hoops to fit through the door frame.

"Well, look at you!" Tammy was standing at the foot of the stairs, camera in hand, snapping away. I had a sudden flashback to junior prom. Only this time my dress was a lot bigger, and I was pretty sure my date wouldn't try to get to second base in the Embassy Suites parking lot. "This is one for the refrigerator!" she continued, a one-woman paparazzi corps. I could feel Dev vogueing behind me. "That's it! Work it, baby! Whoo!" She put down her camera as we stepped off the last stairs onto the hall floor. "Goodness, your clothes are even more amazing in person. Now, come on, thisaway." She walked into the parlor. "I'm so happy I get to pop your sweet tea cherry!"

Dev giggled.

"Is sweet tea different from regular iced tea?" I asked as I attempted to sit on a pink floral sofa. It took me three tries to arrange my hoops in a manner that allowed me to sit behind the mahogany coffee table. A tray laden with a big pitcher of tea, three glasses, and a plate of cookies lay on top of it. Dev perched gingerly at the edge of the couch, as close to the cookies as possible.

"Mmm-hmm." Tammy picked up the pitcher and began pouring glasses. "I'll just let it speak for itself." She handed us each a glass. I took a gulp.

"Whoa!" I exclaimed involuntarily. It was really, *really* sweet.

"Mmm-mmm." Dev smacked his lips. "This might be even better than iced coffee!" he exclaimed, and drained his glass. I wasn't surprised. Dev had yet to meet a caffeinated beverage he didn't like. Or anything that was ever too sweet.

"Come back in a couple years, and I'll make you a pitcher of Alabama Slammers," Tammy said, refilling his glass. "That's *really* better than iced coffee."

"'Alabama Slammers'?" Dev cocked an eyebrow at me. "Sounds like my cup of tea. Or, uh, glass of tea." He took a giant gulp.

"Here, doll, try the coconut pecan shortbread." Tammy nodded toward the plate of cookies.

"Don't mind if I do." Dev gleefully picked up a wedge of shortbread. I demurred, the thought of eating anything in the corset squashed out of me as surely as my capacity for taking deep breaths.

"So . . ." Tammy picked up a cookie, settling in. "Have y'all thought about your story yet?"

"Story?" I asked.

"Pudding, you can't show up unchaperoned, staying with a strange man," Tammy answered, sipping her tea. "It'll ruin your reputation. Well, you'll be fine with most of the reenactors, who acknowledge that they are reenactin', but some of them are real hard-core about it. We've got reenactors who stay in character the whole time, and they won't stand for that. Not one bit."

Dev and I exchanged glances.

"Don't worry about this one's reputation. She's already ruined," Dev said balefully. I elbowed him in the ribs.

"Seriously, what do I do?" I asked.

"Well, you have two options." Tammy munched contemplatively. "One, y'all pretend to be married."

"PFFFF!" Dev snarfed sweet tea out his nose and started laughing uproariously.

"Hey!" I elbowed him again. "You could do a lot worse!"

"Two," Tammy continued, ignoring our squabbling, "y'all pretend to be brother and sister."

"Me and Albino McPasty?" Dev looked skeptical.

"Doesn't matter." Tammy waved around her cookie unconcernedly, before I could object to the pasty comment. "It's all pretend, isn't it? You wanna show up and be the Queen of Sheba, as long as it's the Queen of Sheba in 1861, you're fine. Y'all can be brother and sister if you want to."

"Then brother and sister it is." Dev pulled my hair.

"Ouch!" I rubbed my scalp.

"Just getting in character," he said, taking a second cookie.

Tammy chuckled. We talked until we'd drained the pitcher, and Dev was using his pinkie to pop the last remaining crumbs of shortbread into his mouth.

"We'd best get a move on." Tammy stood and picked up the tray. "Officers'll be just about done, and Beau'll be waitin' on us."

As Tammy took the tray to the kitchen, Dev used one arm to pick up his bag and the other to help me extricate myself from the couch. Tammy pushed two giant cardboard boxes into the living room. I recognized Dev's handwriting on the labels immediately—so *that's* where he shipped the clothes to! In a few minutes, and only with slight difficulty, the three of us and all of our boxes were out of the B&B and back in the minivan.

"I know those hoops take some gettin' used to," Tammy said, as we pulled out of the driveway and I flopped around in back, trying to get comfortable. "You should've seen me at my first reenactment. Like a flounder in a tote bag. But you'll get the hang of it, I promise."

Marbury wasn't far from Pine Level, and in no time at all, we were passing a big granite slab that read CONFEDERATE MEMORIAL PARK. Tammy turned into a gravel parking lot, enclosed by a split-rail fence that was propping up a lone soldier in gray. He looked reminiscent of the cute blob I'd seen from afar in the picture.

"Is that Beau, Tammy?" Dev asked.

"Right on time, bless his heart," Tammy murmured, as she parked, and the soldier straightened up, pushing himself off the fence.

Dev hopped out of the car immediately, rushing to check Beau out under the ruse of extracting me from the back seat.

"Cute!" Dev mouthed appreciatively as he helped me out, and Tammy ran over to give her son a hug.

"Libby! Dev! Y'all come on over," Tammy called, and Dev led me to the fence. "This is my boy, Beau."

I looked up into a pair of startlingly green eyes. Perhaps not uncommon, given the russet tinge to his hair, but they were so vibrantly emerald, they had still surprised me. He was tall, broad shouldered, and classic leading-man handsome. Jaw-droppingly so. But it was actually *his* jaw that had dropped.

"Don't stand there and look all twitterpated—you go on and get their things," Tammy scolded him. "Go on, get." She sighed heavily. "Oh, Lord, you pay him no never mind, Libby. He always was a fool for a pretty girl." Tammy gave Beau a gentle nudge, and they disappeared back behind the minivan.

"Goodness, he looks just like a hotter Tarleton twin, doesn't he?" Dev asked excitedly. I was beginning to get the feeling that the vast majority of Dev's "research" consisted of repeat viewings of *Gone with the Wind.* "I hope he is a Tarleton twin! One for me, one for you." Dev rubbed his hands together.

"Um, I have a boyfriend," I reminded Dev. No well-muscled man in uniform was going to change that.

"No, you don't," Dev replied breezily.

"Dev, you've met him like fifteen times." I rolled my eyes. "You've seen him in his underwear."

"Technically, you don't have a boyfriend," Dev explained. "According to the laws of *Back to the Future,* Garrett McCaffrey, your alleged boyfriend, doesn't even exist. Because he hasn't been born yet. And may never be born if we change the path of history as we know it."

"*Back to the Future* isn't real science. And we didn't actually go back in time," I countered, eyeing him suspiciously. "You know that, right?"

"I'm just saying—what happens in 1861 *stays* in 1861."

chapter two

Unlike Dev, I still believed my boyfriend existed. Even if he hadn't answered his phone last night. Or this morning. I'd sneaked out early, hiding behind the tent in nothing but my pantalets and chemise, because that was all I could put on unassisted. But even after a good fifteen minutes of frantically, furtively dialing, there was still no response.

Last night Beau had moved our small trunks into the tent, before putting our suitcases and the boxes of clothes Dev had shipped to Alabama in the back of his truck. After hugging us goodbye, Tammy had left us in Beau's capable hands. He seemed nice enough, if a bit shy, as he showed us around the camp and into our tent. We'd only unpacked enough stuff to last us for the day, as we'd be leaving the instruction camp for our first battle, and our first selling opportunity, almost immediately. Everything else stayed in the truck. Cars seemed to be the major repositories of anything non-period around here. Well, and the Confederate Memorial Park Visitors Center, of course, which held the major non-period item I was interested in: the bathroom. Everyone else seemed perfectly content to pee in the woods, and while I'd been on enough family camping trips that I didn't have a problem with that, if there was an actual flushing toilet, I was going to use it. However, I had yet to discover a shower anywhere, a situation that was far more troubling.

The camp was a little village of white pup tents, small canvas structures weather-beaten by the sun. Most of the tents were only wide enough for each soldier to place a pallet on the floor, but ours was one of the more luxurious ones, like the officers had. It was big enough to fit two narrow cots with a stack of small trunks containing our day-to-day personal items and clothing between them. Tammy had been kind enough to make sure we had quilts, instead of the scratchy woolen army blankets; two lumpy cotton pillows (another luxury); and a tin pitcher and basin for washing up, which were balanced on top of the stack of trunks. When it was time to go into business, Beau had explained, we'd set up a bigger awning in front of our sleeping tent to display our wares.

"Coffee," Dev moaned, as I slipped back into the tent, sitting up in his cot. "Coffee!" He rubbed his temples.

"Help me get dressed, and we'll go get some." I picked up my corset and held it out to him.

"Uh-uh," he grunted as he got out of bed and stumbled toward me. "Coffee first." He stumbled straight past me and out of the tent, clad in nothing but his cream-colored union suit.

I held my corset under my armpits in the ready position, waiting impatiently. Dev might have been fine wandering around camp in his long underwear, but I wasn't sure I wanted to prance around in front of strangers in nineteenth-century lingerie.

Dev returned a few minutes later, clutching a tin cup. He took a sip, then immediately spat it out, spraying me with a fine mist.

"Eeuw, Dev, gross!" I tried to shield myself from getting coffee on my corset.

"What . . . the hell . . . is that," he said tersely.

"I don't know—coffee?" I brushed little brown drops off my arms. "Oh, gross, gross, gross."

"That"—he pointed an accusing finger at the cup—"is *not* coffee."

"Fine, fine, it's not coffee." I hopped closer, putting my back directly in front of him. "Please help me clothe myself, and we'll figure it out, okay?"

"Okay." Dev nodded, seemingly galvanized into action. "Okay." He put the cup down on top of his trunk. "You stay there, Satan's brew," he instructed the cup, and hurriedly laced me up. I was happy he was preoccupied, because he didn't lace me nearly as tight. As if he were in some sort of nineteenth-century speed-dressing competition, within minutes I was corseted, hoop-skirted, petticoated, and standing in a plaid silk taffeta day dress. Dev chucked a cameo brooch at me to pin on my collar at the base of my throat and flung the tent flap open.

"Mornin', Dev. Libby." Beau was standing outside the tent in gray wool pants, suspenders, and a soft green checked shirt, balancing two tin cups and a plate. He seemed slightly less tongue-tied than he'd been last night. "I fixed you a plate."

"Keep that horse's piss out of my sight," Dev thundered, "or so help me, I will go General Sherman on all of your asses and raze this sorry excuse for a Starbucks to the ground. *Where is the real coffee?!*" Dev pushed his way over to the main ring of campfires.

"Sorry about Dev," I said. I shot Beau an apologetic look and took the plate. "He's really not fit for human companionship before coffee. And thanks for the plate." I smiled. I couldn't believe he'd "fixed me a plate." Just like all the boys wanted to do for Scarlett O'Hara at the Twelve Oaks barbecue! "That was really sweet."

"Wasn't anythin' special." He shrugged. "Besides, I promised my mama I'd take good care of y'all."

He smiled, and I was flooded with warmth that had nothing to do with the Alabama sunshine. Not that it meant anything. I mean, I had a boyfriend. Obviously. Beau was just an infectious smiler. Just friendly, you know. It's always nice to make new friends. Especially ones who smile like they really mean it, with their whole face, reaching all the way up to the startling green of their eyes . . .

"So, what's for breakfast today?" I blushed and looked down at the plate. I had no idea what it was. There was a lump of something fried and yellowish, dusted with a heavy coating of coal black char, next to a little puddle of something sticky.

"Well, today's special is the same as it is every day," Beau said with a laugh. "Johnnycakes."

"Johnnycakes?" I asked. "What are they? And who's Johnny?"

"Nobody really knows, certainly not me," he replied, pushing up the brim of his gray kepi cap to scratch his head. "Some people think it comes from 'journey cakes,' because they pack real well to take on journeys. Others say that it comes from 'Shawnee cakes,' because the Shawnee tribe in the Tennessee Valley came up with 'em. Maybe a slurred version of 'janiken,' which is an Indian word for corn cake. Other people say it comes from 'Johnny Reb,' the nickname for Confederate soldiers, because that's just about all we eat. Except it couldn't be, because people were callin' 'em johnnycakes back during the Revolution. It was real big in Rhode Island, 'specially," he explained. He shook his head. "You think folks'd do their research better."

My jaw dropped. I had never met anyone who knew as much, maybe more, about American culinary history as I did. I'd never even met anyone who was interested in it before.

"And, anyway," he finished, "they're sort of like corn bread."

"Oh, yum! I love corn bread!" I took a big bite and immediately wished I hadn't.

Apparently my distress must have shown on my face, because Beau burst out laughing.

"I said it's *sort of* like corn bread," he clarified. "Except johnnycakes is nothin' but cornmeal, salt, and water. Fried in a skillet over the campfire."

"Oh," I said through a thick mouthful of inedible mush. "Yum."

"Takes some getting used to," he said, fighting valiantly to keep it together, as I kept on chewing what I was 99 percent sure was kindergarten paste. But no matter how much I chewed, it didn't seem to be getting any smaller. "Modern Americans are used to sweeter corn bread. With sugar and flour and stuff. That's why I got you the molasses." He pointed to the little sticky puddle. "You wouldn't have had that back in the 1860s, most likely. Rations were real thin on both sides, but for us especially. Nobody hurt harder than the Southern soldiers. If we were lucky enough to get rations, it would've been just cornmeal probably. Maybe some salt, maybe flour, maybe salt pork—dependin' on how things were goin'. But definitely no sugar. If the troops were lucky enough to run across any sugar or molasses, they would've just dipped the johnnycakes into it, to make it last longer. Bakin' with it thins it out too much."

"Mmm." I swallowed throatily, then took another bite, this time with the molasses. "That's much better."

"Lord, you shoulda seen your face," he said, chuckling. "Hell, I'm givin' you the rest of my molasses. You need it more'n I do."

By this point we'd wandered over to the campfire, where Dev, still in his long underwear, was having a heated discussion with a gaggle of grizzled old men in variations of Confederate uniforms. They were a pretty ragtag bunch. Because the Southern economy was so bad during the war, and the supply lines were so inefficient, soldiers rarely, if ever, received an official Confederate uniform. As the war went on, they were reduced to wearing whatever they could find. Most of the soldiers here were wearing gray pants, albeit in many different shades—some of the pants were more brown than gray, which I remembered learning in a class meant they'd been dyed with butternuts, one of the few things plentifully available in the South. Because of this, "Butternuts" was another nickname for Confederate soldiers. On top, the men wore dirty button-down shirts in all different colors, stripes, and checks. Most of them also had woolen jackets in shades ranging from gray to butternut brown, with the officers' jackets looking more like standard-issue uniforms; but the men were clearly waiting to put them on until absolutely necessary, because of the heat.

"Don't yell at me, yell at the damn Yanks!" one of the old men shouted. "There's no coffee, nor anythin' else! Damn Union naval blockade means everythin's in short supply down here. Food, weapons, machinery, medicine, coffee, everything!"

Beau leaned over to whisper in my ear. "Some of the old-timers like to stay in character the whole time. So to them, there *is* a naval blockade, and that's why we don't have coffee. Not that we just chose not to buy it to be more authentic."

I nodded in understanding and took a bite that was 80 percent molasses, 20 percent johnnycake.

"Before the war," another one said, starting to wax nostalgic, "a pound of beans would have set you back around twenty cents in fed'ral money. But now it's runnin' sixty bucks, Confederate notes. You got sixty bucks hidden in them drawers, boy?"

The rest of the group around the campfire laughed.

"Fine," Dev said tensely. "I get it. There's no coffee. Then what the hell is this?"

From all around the campfire, different men tending pots chimed in with their various coffee substitutes: roasted corn, rye, okra seeds, sweet potatoes, acorns, and peanuts.

"Do any of them," Dev said, rubbing his temples, "contain caffeine?"

Silence.

"I think Bill's still got some yaupon leaves left," one of them eventually piped up. He wore round glasses with thin metal frames and had a bristly brown mustache.

"'Yaupon'?" Dev asked.

"Y'all can make a tea from the leaves of the yaupon shrub. It's a kind of holly. Grows all over. It's got a bit of a kick, but it's hell to digest. I think there's a reason its binomial name is *Ilex vomitoria,*" he concluded sagely.

"He'll be lucky if that's the end it comes out!" one of them roared, and the rest of the soldiers chimed in.

Dev picked up a fresh mug of steaming hot acorns and stomped over to join us. I finished my johnnycakes and set the plate down on an unoccupied stump.

"There was only one surefire way that Southern folks got coffee," Beau suggested.

"Oh?" Dev asked, intrigued.

"Informal truce with the Yanks. During the war, men'd swap tobacco for coffee and run on back before anyone knew they were missin'. Everyone had tobacco."

"Except me," Dev muttered. "But I've got cash, which is better. When do we next see Yanks?"

"Tomorrow." Beau took a swig from his own mug and grimaced slightly at the taste. "Tonight, maybe."

"We're leaving today? Already?" I asked. "We just set everything up!"

"Life of a soldier, always on the move," Beau said, grinning. "We're headin' south to Tannehill. Besides, we've been here all weekend. This wasn't a battle, just trainin' camp. Instruction on firearms, that sort of thing. Get all the new guys up to speed so the others don't call us farby."

Dev shuddered. I was lost.

"'Farby'?" I wrinkled my nose, confused.

"Didn't you research *anything?*" Dev sighed with mock exasperation. "'Farb' is a derogatory term used in the hobby of historical reenacting in reference to participants who exhibit indifference to historical authenticity, either from a material-cultural standpoint or in action. It can also refer to the inauthentic materials used by those reenactors,'" Dev quoted prosaically. *"Wikipedia."*

"While normally I don't condone *Wikipedia* as a valid

source," Beau drawled, and my heart skipped a beat—finally someone who took checking the validity of their source material *seriously!*—"in this case, it's pretty accurate. Farbs are reenactors who don't care about bein' authentic, not with their uniforms or accessories, or even the way they act. We take bein' authentic real serious in this regiment. We don't even let women in, which a lot of the regiments do. Let women dress up as soldiers an' fight, I mean," he clarified, nodding at me. "I don't have a problem with it, but most of the older crowd think it's too farby."

"And being a farb is like social *suicide,*" Dev added. "Major no-no. There's no better way to get blacklisted than to be a farby sutler."

"'S true," Beau agreed. "It'll sink your business like Mike DuBose sank the Tide back in 2000."

Dev and I stared at him blankly.

"The Alabama Crimson Tide?" he tried. "Finished three and eight that season?" Still nothing. "Football?"

"Ahhh," we said in unison, nodding.

"Yeah, no," Dev said. "We don't do that."

"Anyway," Beau said, shaking his head, "y'all have nothing to worry about. From what I can see"—he looked me up and down, eyes coming to rest on mine as he smiled warmly—"everything looks amazing."

I blushed, but before I could formulate a response, a small bear pushed its way between us and started attacking my tin plate.

"Aw, Willie, no!" Beau moaned, and tried to pull him off. On closer inspection, it turned out not to be a bear, but a very large, very happy, cocoa-colored dog. "I hope you were done with your molasses." He grinned ruefully. "I swear that dog has some kind of radar system that lets him know when anyone in Alabama sets down a plate."

Dev watched, horrified, as the dog joyously cleaned the plate with a massive pink tongue. "What on earth is that . . . that . . . that creature?"

"That"—Beau folded his arms proudly—"is Willie. He's a Chessie, mostly. A Chesapeake Bay retriever," he explained. "But there's definitely somethin' else in there."

"Like grizzly?" Dev said tartly.

Willie finished licking the plate and looked up happily, tongue lolling.

"Hey, boy," I said, kneeling down, and Willie came galumphing over.

"You're not going to . . . touch that beast, are you?" Dev was all disbelief.

"Sure am." I scratched his ears, and Willie barked happily.

"Aw, he likes you," Beau said softly.

"I bet he likes pretty much everybody. Don't you, boy?" He barked again, in the affirmative. "He probably also likes that I have molasses all over my hands."

"You a dog person, then?" Beau knelt down to join me.

"Oh, definitely. I love dogs." Willie slobbered happily. "We have two back home. Both much smaller than this guy." I grinned. "But then again, most dogs are."

"Corporal Anderson!" someone shouted from off in the distance.

"Duty calls." Beau straightened and stood. "Let me see what he wants, and I'll be right back."

Beau headed off, Willie loping along behind him. I stood too, and came face to face with Dev, whose eyebrows were up to his hairline.

"What?" I asked blankly.

"So now that you've cleaned up the whole dog versus cat issue, have you decided on two kids or three?" he said archly.

"What are you talking about?"

"Why, Miss Libby, I do decla-uh, I hate that there *Wikipedia,* and I love me some obscu-ah nahn-teenth-cent'ry hist'ry." Dev parodied Beau in a ridiculously over-the-top southern accent. "Let's git mah-rrried and have lots of bay-bies and raise giant daawwwgs."

"Oh, shut your face." I shoved him playfully. "He was *not* like that. He likes me as a friend. As a person. Just like he likes you."

"Ah have nev-uh seen such a vision in a corset and hoop skurt. Y'all are as purty as a speckled pup."

"We're friends. Just friends. Just because your depraved mind can't fathom the fact that people who could hypothetically be attracted to each other, even though they aren't, can be *just friends,*" I said, trying to keep talking over him.

"Ah'm so gallant and charmin' and chivalrous and han'som' in mah uni-fahhhm, and y'all are mah soooul-maaayte." Dev pretended to swoon.

"And, anyway, I have a boyfriend," I concluded triumphantly.

"Whom you still haven't mentioned to Corporal Hotpants." Dev sipped his coffee demurely. "Interesting."

"It's not interesting!" I protested. "I just don't want to be one of those girls who's like, 'Hi, I'm Libby. I have a boyfriend!'

the minute you meet them! It's super annoying! You might as well go ahead and print it on a T-shirt or something."

"I shouldn't have unleashed you on the world in that corset." Dev shook his head. "You're a danger to society. It's not fair to the hetero *sapiens*. They can't help themselves."

"Seriously, stop," I chided him. "Nothing would ever happen with Beau. Not in a million years. Garrett is the best boyfriend ever. Even if he hasn't returned any of my calls. Or texts. And has apparently forgotten I exist."

Before Dev could form a rebuttal, Corporal Hotpants himself reappeared, accompanied by a middle-aged man in a long gray officer's jacket.

"So this must be the little lady I've heard so much about." He picked up my hand, bent down, and kissed it, the whiskers of his full-on muttonchops scratching the back of my hand. "Now I understand what all the fuss was about."

Beau blushed, which brought out the red in his hair. "Uh, L-Libby," he stammered, "I mean Miss . . . Miss . . ."

"Kelting," I supplied.

"Miss Kelting. This is Captain Cauldwell." The older man bowed. "Captain Cauldwell, Miss Kelting."

"It is truly a pleasure." I think Captain Cauldwell smiled, but it was hard to tell under the bushy mustache. "Good to have a woman around. Gives the boys somethin' to look at."

I smiled awkwardly. That was nice, I guess . . . if a little sexist. Dev coughed. Loudly.

"And this is . . ." Beau turned to Dev and realized he had no idea what his last name was.

"Mr. Ravipati," Dev answered.

Captain Cauldwell looked back and forth between us.

"He's my brother," I explained hurriedly, just in case the captain was one of the hard-core, serious 24/7 in-character types. Captain Cauldwell raised an eyebrow. "Uh, half-brother," I amended.

"And sutler to the stars. At your service." Dev bowed with a flourish.

"Ah, that's right. Mrs. Anderson spoke real highly of y'all," Captain Cauldwell said, nodding. "You make that dress?" He indicated my outfit, and Dev nodded his consent. "Those're some good-lookin' duds."

Beau shot us a discreet thumbs-up. Apparently, we were in.

"Thanks ever so." Dev fluttered his eyelashes.

"Now I'm in charge of this unit," the captain continued. "So if y'all need anythin', have any problems, y'all let me know. Not that you will. Have any problems, that is." He clapped a hand on Beau's shoulder. "Beau here's promised to look after y'all, and he's a good kid." Beau glowed under his praise. "Brought him into the unit myself, and up through the ranks, so I know what I'm talkin' about. Corporal Anderson!" he barked suddenly, all business.

"Yes, sir!" Beau saluted.

"Facilitate camp breakdown. I want us ready to move!" He touched his hat and bowed slightly. "Ma'am."

"We don't have to move anything, do we?" Dev asked, horrified, once Captain Cauldwell was out of earshot.

"Naw, but you might want to put somethin' on over those drawers." Beau smirked.

Dev had clearly completely forgotten he was in his underwear. To be fair, I had too.

"Just get your things together. I have to help the rest of the guys break down, and then I'll load y'all into my truck."

"Corporal Anderson!" someone yelled. "You gonna finish your tea party, or you gonna help us pack?"

Beau rolled his eyes, grinning. "I'll be back."

He jogged off, and Dev and I started wandering back to our tent.

"'Gives the boys somethin' to look at,'" Dev muttered. "What am I, chopped liver?"

"No, you're a crazy man wandering around in long underwear," I answered, giving him a look.

"You'd think they'd never seen a girl before," he sniffed.

"Well, I am the only one here," I said.

"According to *The Story the Soldiers Wouldn't Tell,* there should be way more gays," he complained.

"But they wouldn't tell." We stepped into the tent. "Maybe they are gay, but they're just not telling."

"Good call," he said, and pulled on a white cotton twill three-piece frock suit. "New mission: gayhunt."

"That sounds like some kind of hate crime."

"You know what I mean." He casually tied a green silk cravat in a loose, floppy bow. "This'll be our new mission at the battlefield. Check out all the other soldiers in different units and spot the gays. It's probably best not to dip one's nib in the office ink, anyway. Or the unit ink, as it were."

"Definitely best," I agreed, as Dev checked out his reflection and picked up a white broad-brimmed hat.

"You like?" He struck three model poses. "Jeff Davis had one just like it."

"You and the former president of the Confederate States of America are on a nickname basis?" I asked.

"'Jefferson' is just too stuffy," he said with a smirk. "Here." He handed me a wide-brimmed straw hat trimmed with a taffeta plaid ribbon that matched my skirt. "Seashore hat, Godey's, 1861. Gotta protect that porcelain complexion."

"Mmm."

Once the few things we'd brought with us were back in our trunks, we headed out of the tent, and I was certainly glad I had that hat. The Alabama sun was beating down brutally. Dev and I sat on some rocks at the edge of the camp and watched as the soldiers swarmed around, breaking down the camp. I popped up and offered to help at one point, but was firmly escorted back to my seat by a group of men who informed me that a pretty little thing like me had no business lifting a finger, and they weren't gonna stand by and let a lady work in the hot sun. So Dev and I waited and chatted in the sunshine, until, much later, all of the tents were dismantled and packed into modern cars and trucks. Once everything was settled, Beau came to collect us, Willie padding along in his wake.

"Sorry that took so long," Beau said. He reached out his hand and helped me up. "My truck's right this way." He held out his arm to escort me, and although I was surprised at the gesture, I wasn't altogether displeased. There was something to this whole chivalry thing, after all. I took his arm, and we walked to the parking lot, Dev trailing grumpily behind like an unwilling third wheel.

We stopped at the passenger side of an old red pickup truck. Beau opened the door for me and helped me up. I folded my hoops into the seat. Once Beau saw that I was safely in, he crossed around to the driver's seat.

"Ah, a classic. The 1993 Dodge Dakota," Dev said quietly. "You sure don't choose your men for their rides."

I kicked him with a dainty booted heel as he scrambled into the cab of the truck. With Beau plus the two of us, and me in my hoop skirt, it was pretty close quarters. Willie sat patiently in the driveway, looking up at us.

"Is that beast coming in?" Dev asked, appalled. "I'm wearing a *white suit!* He better not sit on me. This outfit is not supposed to come with a fur coat. You're terribly out of season, ducky," he addressed the dog.

"He can sit on me. Here, Willie!" I patted my lap, and Willie clambered up and over Dev—who moaned with dismay—finally settling on my lap. He was so big it was smothering but nice. Willie's tail wagged happily, smacking Dev repeatedly in the nose.

Packed nice and tightly, we set off.

"Are we there yet?" Dev whined the minute we passed the sign thanking us for visiting Confederate Memorial Park.

"Not quite," Beau said, as we barreled down the road. Tammy was right—he did drive fast—and with breezy, one-handed confidence. "It's a little less than two hours to Tuscaloosa."

"I thought we were going somewhere called Tannehill?" I asked.

"We are." Beau sped by and passed another car. "Tannehill Ironworks Historical State Park. It's about halfway between Birmingham and Tuscaloosa. There's more than fifteen hundred acres for us to set up and fight on, which is good, since we got more than five hundred reenactors last year."

"Excellent," Dev said, rubbing his hands together. "'The

best things in life are free,'" he sang, "'but you can keep them for the birds and bees. Now give me money.'"

Willie whined.

"My voice isn't *that* bad," Dev broke off, offended. "Everyone's a critic."

"Now, Willie," Beau reprimanded him, jokingly. "Be nice to our guests."

"Stuck with the Simon Cowell of dogs," Dev complained. "And he's the size of Randy."

Beau and I chatted as we sped north to Tuscaloosa. Dev had fallen asleep almost immediately, as he was wont to do when in a moving vehicle. His head lolled against the window, a faint trickle of drool working its way down his chin as he snored softly.

"How'd you get into this?" I asked. "Reenacting, I mean."

"It was my mama's idea," Beau said with a grin. "My dad passed away when I was real young—"

"Oh, I'm—I'm so sorry," I interrupted, the words burbling up before I could stop them.

"No, it's, uh, it's fine." He smiled tensely, something shuttered flitting across his eyes. "But my mama thought I could use some positive male role models. So she signed me up as a drummer boy. Jeff—uh, Captain Cauldwell—had been a poker buddy of my dad's. So he sorta looked after me, taught me the ropes, well . . . They all sorta did. It's a real close group. They all look out for their own. Sorta gruff, not the friendliest, always suspicious about newbies . . . They haven't been too rough on ya, have they?" he asked anxiously.

"No, no, they're fine," I assured him. "Just not super outgoing."

"Yeah, they probably won't pay you much notice, but I wouldn't worry about it." He shrugged. "It's just their way. Prefer to keep to themselves. And, anyway . . . well . . . more'n ten years later . . . here I am."

"That's cool that you stuck with it for so long."

"Well, I love history," he said, and colored a bit, embarrassed. "I mean, to do this, you have to. And if you're a big ol' history nerd, like me, it doesn't get better than this." He grinned. "But I'm guessin' you already know that. Or you wouldn't be sittin' in this truck in 150-year-old underwear."

"So true." I grinned back. "It's hard to explain to other people, isn't it? How much you love it."

"I s'pose," he said. "Although I s'pose I'm lucky, spendin' my summers here with people who are even nuttier about the war than I am, and then at UA . . . Y'all have Phi Alpha Theta at your school?"

"What?" I asked skeptically. "What is that, a frat? I, um, haven't started college yet."

"You're still in high school?" Beau asked, surprised. "'Cause you don't look—"

"Just graduated," I interrupted him. "I'm starting college in the fall." Beau nodded. "But I have to say I find it really hard to believe that you sit around with your frat brothers discussing the effects of the Union naval blockade on the Confederate home front or whatever."

"No, not a frat," Beau said, roaring with laughter. "Phi Alpha Theta is a history honors society."

"Oh." I blushed.

"Check and see if they have it at your school when you start, then. It's nice, to have that group. Whole buncha nerds together." He smiled. "And the department at UA's pretty good too—I can concentrate in exactly what I want to study."

"Which is . . . ?" I prompted, even though I had a pretty good idea what he was going to say.

"American Civilization to 1865, History of Alabama to 1865, American South to 1865, U.S. Constitution to 1865, the Coming of the Civil War, the Civil War, Mexican War through Civil War . . ." He rattled off the course names.

"I'm sensing a pattern," I teased.

"Funny," he said, and laughed. "All right, smarty-pants, what is it you wanna study when you start next year?"

"American social history, definitely. Probably eighteenth- and nineteenth-century women's and gender studies," I replied.

"Gotcha," he mused. "So we're in the same general area, just comin' at the same thing from two different sides. Pretty much."

"Pretty much."

"Coffee." Dev woke himself up with a start, snorting a little. "Coffee," he murmured, and snorted again, rubbing his eyes. "Oh, I had the most horrible nightmare." He sighed. "I was stuck in a terrible land without coffee. And you were there, and you, and you!" he said, as he channeled Dorothy from the *Wizard of Oz,* pointing at me and Beau and Willie, in turn. "Wait a minute . . . that wasn't a dream, was it?"

"'Fraid not," Beau replied cheerily.

"You are altogether too chipper for someone with no caffeine in his system." Dev glared at him. "I want coofffeeeee," he cried softly into his seat belt.

"Well, turns out, you're in luck," Beau said. He took the next exit and pulled off the highway. "We're almost there. And

I'm gonna need to fill up on gas before we stop. And I'm pretty sure the gas station'll have coffee."

We were almost there? I couldn't believe how fast the time had flown by.

As we pulled into the gas station, Dev wept tears of joy.

"I think that I shall never see a poem as lovely as a BP," he recited. "Hello, lover," he cooed at the yellow sunburst on the big green BP sign.

Dev was out of the truck before it had come to a complete stop. He sprinted into the mini-mart without a backwards glance.

"Comin'?" Beau asked as he hopped out.

"Nah, I'm fine," I said, gesturing to my hoops. "With all of this, you'll be done pumping gas by the time I get out of the truck." Plus, I wasn't exactly sure how I felt about hanging around a gas station just outside of Tuscaloosa in the twenty-first century wearing nineteenth-century clothing.

"Suit yourself." Beau clearly had no such worry as he stood around pumping gas like a Confederate pep boy. He tipped his gray kepi hat to the other people at the gas station, who didn't seem to think it was anything out of the ordinary.

And then, when I had finally stopped thinking about it, my phone vibrated. I scrambled around through what felt like a million yards of muslin, until I triumphantly extracted my cell phone from where I'd stashed it in my corset.

"Garrett!" I cried. "Finally! Where are you? What's up? How are you? How's it going?"

"Hey, Libby," he said, and sighed, almost dejectedly. "What's with all the questions? I thought I was the reporter."

I smiled. It was sort of a halfhearted joke, but at least he seemed a little bit more like himself.

"Very funny, Mr. Hotshot Reporter." I shifted under Willie's weight. "So do you spend more of your time running around chasing hot leads and yelling, 'Stop the presses!' or just coming up with brilliant bons mots behind a big glossy desk?"

"Um . . . not exactly." He laughed mirthlessly. "I-don't-even-have-a-desk," he mumbled very quietly.

"Sorry, what? What was that?" I asked. I had no idea what he'd said.

"I don't have a desk!" He shouted so loudly I nearly dropped the phone, and Willie barked unhappily. "I don't even have a desk," Garrett repeated at a normal volume.

"Well, okay," I said, commiserating, "that's not great, I guess, but—"

"I thought I'd at least have a cubicle," he said sadly, "or something. It didn't have to be fancy. It's not like I was expecting an *office* or something ridiculous. I just thought I'd have a desk. At least access to a desk. A time-share to a desk maybe, but no." He sighed again, heavily. "No. I have to sit on the floor."

"The . . . the floor?"

"They had to do major cutbacks because of the economy," Garrett said bitterly. "And they replaced everyone they let go with interns. So they don't have to pay them. Or provide things like desks. And there's so many of us, we have to sit on the floor. It's . . . not great."

"Oh, Garrett," I said, frowning. "I'm so sorry. I know how much you were looking forward to this, and this isn't exactly what you pictured—"

"Definitely not," he said grimly. "But I'm trying to get sent out on assignment. I just need the right story. So hopefully I can get sent closer to—"

"Regardez!" Dev shouted, as he flung open the door and proudly held up a bucket-size coffee. "Mmm." He held it under my nose. "Smell that. Liquid nirvana. Mmm." He took another sip. "This coffee is awful. But at least it's not yams."

"Is that Dev?" Garrett asked over the phone.

"Yep," I confirmed.

Beau finished filling up the tank and started getting back in the truck.

"Is that loverboy?" Dev asked as he sat back down.

"Mmm-hmm." Out of the corner of my eye, I happened to catch a glimpse of Beau, whose face fell.

"Tell snookums I say hi." Dev made a kissy face as he blew on his hot coffee.

"Dev says hi," I said quickly. "Listen, I have to go; we're getting back on the road."

"Marching to the sea, General Sherman?" Garrett cracked. "Oh, no, wait—you're the enemy."

"Har-har." I rolled my eyes. "With wit like that, you'll shoot straight to the top in no time. But seriously," I said softly, "I know this sucks. But it'll get better. You'll be okay."

"I know." Garrett sighed. "I love you, Libby."

"I love you too."

I hung up and stuck the phone back in my corset as Beau started the car.

"So . . . that your boyfriend?" Beau peeled out of the gas station so fast he burned rubber.

"Mmm-hmm." I held on to Willie for dear life as Beau

turned corners at breakneck speed, tires kicking up gravel. Dev raised an eyebrow over the rim of his giant coffee as he balanced it, careful not to spill a single precious drop, no matter how fast we were going.

"He back up north?"

"Yeah." I knotted my fingers deeper into Willie's fur. "He's working at a newspaper. In Boston."

"Nice. Nice." Beau nodded tensely. "Real nice."

Thankfully, we really were almost at the state park. Probably because we were traveling at the speed of light. We managed to arrive in one piece, albeit one slightly frazzled piece, as the truck skidded to a stop in the parking lot, kicking up a hailstorm of dust and gravel.

"Aw, hell no," Beau said with dismay. "Randall."

I followed his gaze. A bit of a ways into the park, there stood a group of boys in Confederate uniforms, most of whom looked to be between ten and fourteen, in a very straight line.

"School must've gotten out." Beau pulled a frown. "Dammit."

"Um, who are they?" I asked.

"Boy Scout Troop 72. They spend the summer with us, earnin' some kind of history or military badge or somethin'."

"Aw, that's so cute!" I exclaimed.

Beau shot me a look. "You'll see," he said, as he got out of the truck. He waited for Dev and Willie to scramble out before helping me. "Oh, how quickly you'll learn."

Dev had miraculously finished that enormous coffee during the quick drive. He expertly tossed his cup into a trash can at the edge of the parking lot.

"We'd better get this over with," Beau said, offering me

his arm, and together we walked toward the Boy Scouts. Dev sauntered along on my other side, trying to ignore Willie, who was desperately clamoring for his attention.

"Corporal Anderson." A skinny, pasty scout at the head of the line stepped forward and saluted him.

"At ease, Randall." Beau sighed.

"You can't make me!" Randall shot back. "Uh, I mean, you don't outrank me, soldier."

"I think I do, Brevet Corporal," Beau said, and sighed again.

"Think again, Second Corporal," Randall retorted.

Beau shot me a look as if to say, *See what I mean?* And I did. Randall seemed to be an extremely whiny and obnoxious specimen of twelve-year-old boy.

"Does it matter, Randall?"

"I'm telling Captain Cauldwell." Randall's nostrils flared. "I'm telling him that you don't respect rank and . . . and . . . I'm telling."

"Aw, come on, Randall, not again."

Randall stared Beau down for a minute, then fled in toward the camp.

"Come on, Randall, you don't need to bother him with this—he's busy with registration and stuff!" Beau yelled after him. "Aw, hell." He ran his hands through his hair. "I'd better go deal with this before he pisses off the captain."

Beau chased him off, leaving me and Dev alone with the Boy Scouts.

"Excuse me, ma'am." A boy who looked like he should have had his own Disney Channel original series—complete with a *Hannah Montana* crossover special—stepped out of line. "Allow me to introduce myself. I'm Cody. Now, would you say you're a Civilian Youth?"

"Um . . ." I looked to Dev for an answer. "Yes?"

"Well, I am the Civilian Youth Coordinator. And darlin'"—he looked me up and down—"I would love to coordinate you."

"Good Lord," I said, and stared at him in disbelief. "What are you, thirteen?"

"Fourteen," he retorted, bristling. "And this Boy Scout is all man."

Dev snorted. I looked over, and he was red in the face, shaking with silent laughter.

"You got a name, sweet thing?"

"It's Libby. And you need to, um, take it down a notch, buster," I added for extra emphasis.

Dev mouthed, "Buster?" and laughed harder.

"Didja know the Scout motto is 'Do a good turn daily'? I bet I could do you a good turn. Daily."

Good Lord. I looked to Dev for help, but he was way too amused by the whole thing to step in and offer any assistance.

"Allow me to appoint myself as your personal . . . very personal . . . *body*guard." He winked. "Emphasis on *body.*"

"Yeah, I got that, thanks." I grimaced. "But I really don't think I need a bodyguard."

"Aw, sure you do, honey." Cody's grin widened. "Who all do you think's gonna protect you from the ghost?"

"Ghost?" Dev spat. "You have *got* to be kidding me."

chapter three

"If I had known," Dev complained, yanking my corset strings, "that you were going to turn out to be some kind of freaky Jennifer Love Hewitt *Ghost Whisperer* paranormal magnet"—another yank—"I swear to God I would've sat next to someone else at lunch in ninth grade." Yank.

"Ow, stop pulling so hard!" I whimpered. "Stop trying to punish me with my own underwear! It's not my fault! I didn't know there would be a ghost! Plus, it was *your* idea to come here!" I concluded triumphantly.

Dev ignored that remark and yanked so hard I nearly lost my balance.

"Whoopsie!" Cody gleefully poked his head between our tent flaps. "Oh me, oh my, I seem to have the wrong tent!"

"CODY!" I shrieked. "OUT!"

"Oh my goodness, I am just so embarrassed." He grinned. "So terribly, terribly sorry. What an unfortunate, yet innocent, mistake."

"That was neither innocent nor a mistake!" I fumed. "Dev, what did I say about tying the tent flaps closed!" I tried to get close enough to kick Cody, but Dev, who was holding on to my corset strings, reined me in. I was completely immobilized. "Get out, get out, GET OUT!"

"No, come on in, tiny pervert." Dev crooked a finger. "I must needs speak with thee."

"He can't come in!" I flailed around, utterly in vain, as Cody sauntered into the tent and took a seat on my cot. "Don't invite him in—it's like inviting in a vampire! You're not supposed to do it! Then you're doomed!"

"Oh, stop being such a prude," Dev scolded. "This is silly. You're wearing more than you would at the beach."

"Unfortunately," Cody said lustily.

I glared.

"You pay for the privilege of your presence with information, gremlin," Dev said, as he tied my excruciatingly tight corset with a neat bow.

"What all do you want to know, Grandpa?" Cody leaned back, clearly enjoying himself.

"I'm going to ignore that ageist comment, you prepubescent toe rag," Dev commented, as he helped me into my hoops. "I want to know about the ghost."

Last night, before Cody had elaborated on the ghost he'd referred to, Randall had returned and marshaled all the Boy Scouts away. The entire camp, which was much bigger this time, had transformed into a flurry of activity, so we hadn't had another opportunity to ask anyone about it. It had taken all night for the three hundred and something Confederate soldiers from reenactment units all over the South to set up their tents at one side of the field, and for the Union forces on the other side to do the same. There were more than five hundred reenactors sprawled out over the fields of the Tannehill Ironworks Historical State Park, and they stretched out into a seemingly endless sea of tiny tents. Beau and some of the other men had set up our tent on Sutlers' Row, which was on a little hill overlooking the large field where the battle would take place. We were neatly sandwiched into a little lane of other sutlers, all with sleeping tents behind and awnings for selling out front, between a millinery shop and a sock specialist.

"Ahh, that." Cody exhaled. "Guess your precious Corporal Anderson didn't tell you he's cursed, then."

"Whaa?" I exclaimed, muffled by muslin, as Dev slipped a petticoat over my head.

"You heard me. Cursed. So I'd keep away from that boy's bad juju, baby doll."

"I have no intention of going near Corporal Anderson's juju, bad or otherwise," I said primly.

Dev snorted as he helped me into my dress—today's was a sheer white lawn dimity confection with little puff sleeves and a sweetheart neckline, soft and light as a cloud.

"Talk, gremlin," Dev prompted.

"Righty-o, Gramps. Well, our story takes place right before the war broke out, in the foothills of Mount Sterling." Cody's voice had taken on a hushed, mysterious quality, as though it was midnight around a campfire, instead of eight a.m. in a muslin tent. "There lived a girl named Anne Mitchell, a girl so beautiful they called her the 'belle of Central Kentucky.' Now me, I prefer blondes"—he winked at me—"but if the brunette thing floats your boat, then—"

"Less editorializing," I said, grimacing.

"Fine, fine," he continued. "So, this Anne babe was like Megan Fox hot, and she fell for this guy named John Bell Hood. They were passionately, completely, totally in love. And even when he went off to West Point, they promised themselves to each other. However, as soon as old Hood was out the door, a new guy showed up on the scene—remembered only as 'Mr. Anderson.'"

Cody raised an eyebrow meaningfully, as did Dev.

"Now, even though Anne was having none of it, still bein' totally into Hood, her family preferred Anderson," Cody continued with relish. "Anderson was crazy rich, so her family pressured her into marrying him. Anne managed to send a letter to Hood at West Point, tellin' him what was happenin', and no matter what, she'd love him *forever.* Like even from beyond the grave," he said, his voice dropping a few octaves. "Hood got the letter"—his voice returned to normal—"immediately left West Point, and rode hell for leather to Kentucky. Somehow they made this secret plan to run away and elope, but one of the Mitchell slaves discovered Anne was missing like a minute after she left and raised the alarm. Anne's father and brothers caught her real quick and locked her in her room until the day she married Anderson."

"She married him? Anderson?" I asked, totally caught up in the story.

"That she did." Cody nodded. "But even after she was married, she refused to leave her room. She was super depressed and still totally bananas for Hood. And then when she found out she was pregnant, she stopped speaking altogether. Until, that is, the day that little Corwin Anderson was born"—Cody's voice dropped to a whisper, and Dev and I leaned in—"and she spoke her first words in nine months. And with those words she laid a curse 'upon all who had any part in making me marry Anderson when my heart will always belong to John Bell Hood.'"

"Did anything happen?" Dev whispered.

"Did it? Aw, hell, sure as I'm sittin' here. Not even an hour after the birth of lil Corwin, the sky began to darken, a strange thunderstorm came to rest over the Mitchell house—an' before you knew it, the house was struck by a bolt of lightning, killin' Anne, her brother, and the slave girl who told when Anne had run."

"Oooh," Dev murmured.

"So what does this have to do with Beau?" I asked skeptically. "This all happened like 150 years ago. Doesn't mean Beau's cursed. He didn't have any part in forcing Anne to marry his great-great-great-grandfather or whatever."

"You might think that," Cody said, raising a hand for silence. "But, in fact, the curse has dogged the Anderson family, plaguing them with strange and violent deaths as the years have passed."

"Didn't Tammy say her husband, Mr. Anderson, had passed away?" Dev asked, quietly, fearfully.

"Yes, but that doesn't mean—"

"Yep, just kept gettin' weirder as time went on," Cody continued. "Anne's grandson English Anderson killed his brother with a brick, gave his father a heart attack, and was eventually stoned to death."

"Oh my God," I gasped.

"Then after Judson Anderson committed suicide in the forties, the Andersons who remained alive left Kentucky to try to escape the curse—and, well, they ended up in Alabama." Cody raised his eyebrow again.

"Did it work?" I asked.

"Didn't seem to, as Anne Mitchell's ghost now stalks the last male descendant of the man who done her wrong—one Corporal Beauregard Anderson," Cody concluded with ghoulish relish.

"Eep!" Dev said.

"I don't believe it," I stated flatly. "There isn't a ghost stalking Beau, out for vengeance. That's ridiculous."

"Wait and see," Cody replied, and shrugged.

"Ridiculous," I said again, placing my hands on my hips. "We don't have time for any of this nonsense." I was trying to be business-like, but taking charge in lawn dimity is hard. "The camp opens to the public at nine o'clock, and we"—I looked meaningfully at Dev—"have a lot of work to do. And you," I said, glaring at Cody, "probably have Civilian Youths to harass somewhere."

"Yes, ma'am." Cody jumped up, snapped to attention, and saluted. "Now, some folks may not like a take-charge woman, but, darlin', you could boss me around all day."

"Move!" I barked, and he did, Dev trailing somewhat sheepishly behind.

"Matter of fact, I have a most important job," Cody announced proudly as we exited the tent. He picked up a stack of thick plastic sheets that he must have left outside the tent before beginning his whole peeping Tom routine. "Signage!" He held one up. It said CIVIL WAR above a bright red arrow.

"Nice sign." Dev arched an eyebrow.

"Aw, man, don't hate the playah, hate the game," Cody said, and shoved all the signs under his arm. "I've gotta go pound these babies into the ground. Latah, hatahs." Cody used his free hand to salute with two fingers before trudging up the hill that marked the edge of the camp. Sometime this morning, an unidentified pristine white tent had sprung up just past its borders. It was far too shiny to be plain muslin, and there was a sign hammered into the ground in front of it. Squinting, I could just make out "Dixie Acres." Or at least that's what I thought I saw.

"That can't be good," Dev said, once Cody reached the top of the hill and stopped in front of the new tent. A guy in a crisply pressed modern suit emerged from the tent and began arguing with Cody, who was gesticulating wildly with one of his signs.

"I know," I said, and started pulling sample dresses out of our trunks, hastily hanging them on the rack at the front of the tent. "What do you think they're fighting about?"

"No, not that." Dev folded his arms contemplatively, drumming his fingers on his elbows. "I meant the undead hottie stalking Corporal Hotpants."

"Okay, one, a little help here?" I struggled under the surprisingly heavy weight of yards of muslin. Dev ambled over and started helped me hang things. "Two, stop calling him Corporal Hotpants. You know his name. And, three, you're being ridiculous. There's no undead hotties, or undead notties, for that matter. There's no undead anything. Ghosts don't exist."

"Um, yes, they do." Dev vigorously shook a wrinkle out of an emerald-green taffeta number. "I saw one last summer."

"That wasn't a ghost!" I said exasperatedly. "That was an asshole with a white suit! You know it wasn't a ghost. We caught him."

"It was still scary," Dev replied stubbornly. "I'm officially mad at you."

"What? Me? Why?"

"OMG, what was that show on the Disney Channel? With the girl who, like, lived on a tour bus and was always running into ghosts?" Dev tapped his foot, thinking.

"I don't know! Why are you mad at me?"

"That's *So Weird*!" he shouted.

"What's so weird?" I wrinkled my nose.

"Um, no, hello, blond moment, the show. It was called *So Weird*. And you're just like that girl. A weird scary ghost magnet. This is totally your fault."

"It is *not* my fault, and I am *not* a ghost magnet! You're the one who brought us here! Who picked the Fifteenth Alabama? Not me!"

"It was totally your energy that drew me to it," he insisted.

"If you want to focus on something not good, focus on this," I suggested. "Where on earth are we supposed to shower? It's been a couple days. That is way too long. And I haven't even seen a hint of a shower."

"Many reenactors go for months at a time without showering," Dev said grimly. "Authenticity."

"I sincerely hope we are not those reenactors." Months without showering? No way. There were limits to my authenticity. Very defined limits.

"I smuggled in enough AXE to mask the scent of a decomposing body," Dev said with a set jaw. "Or a very dirty historical reenactor. Just in case."

"Oh, God," I said, blanching.

"But I would much rather take a shower. We'll figure it out. I'll ask Corporal Hotpants when he shows up again."

We continued talking about ghosts, showers, and AXE as we finished displaying the dresses. They hung on two poles at opposite ends of the awning in front of our sleeping tent, and we had a table in between from which to conduct business. Dev went out to double-check, for the millionth time this morning, that the stake for our CONFEDERATE COUTURE sign (with a red, white, and blue logo of Dev's own creation) was hammered into the ground in a perfectly perpendicular line, so the sign hung straight.

The camp opened to the public at nine, but the battle didn't start until two, which gave us plenty of time to sell, sell, sell. Practically the minute our tent flaps were open for business, we were swamped. Our regiment may not have had any women in it (well, except for me—sort of), but nearly all of the other ones did. Most had many women, typically the wives and girlfriends of enlisted men, who portrayed their wives and girlfriends in period costume. And it seemed as though they had all descended on our tent.

I hadn't seen Dev spring to life like this since the Skate Canada International Men's Figure Skating Reserve Team came to St. Paul for the International Skating Union Junior Grand Prix. He was a whirlwind of fitting, trimming and pinning patterns, and making sure he had every measurement so the finished product would fit exquisitely. I stood behind the table, collecting checks and making change, watching as Dev's D&G-labeled future crystallized from a dream into reality. If we kept up at the rate we were going, Dev would even be able to afford those miniature Hermès dominoes he'd had his eye on. I couldn't quite fathom the appeal of designer dominoes, but whatever made him happy . . .

"We are now only thirty minutes away from the start of the battle!" a voice boomed out over a PA system. They'd been making periodic announcements all day, mostly counting down the minutes until the battle, and I still had no idea where the voice was coming from. "Make sure you step on down to Colonel Jon's Kitchen for some delicious Indian fry bread before we get goin'! Settle yourself down in a shady spot with a nice, cold glass of homemade root beer, courtesy of Colonel Robert's Homemade Elixirs, and prepare to witness history!"

"Why aren't we by the food sutlers?" Dev complained from down by my ankles, where he was measuring the hemline for the very short wife of an officer in the Fourteenth Ohio. "I heard they have kettle corn."

"Scoot, scoot!" Something large and magenta was pushing its way toward us. "Yes, I mean scoot, Mabel, and I mean you, too! Did you not hear the man, half an hour! Give these kids a break! They'll still be here after the battle. Y'all can buy all you want then, Mabel, for Pete's sake."

Tammy Anderson, resplendent in a shiny taffeta dress, elbowed a skinny woman in plaid out of the way until she stood before us, clicking her tongue in exasperation at poor Mabel.

"Tammy!" Dev cried delightedly. He finished his measurements and sprung neatly to his feet. "All set, ma'am. Please pay my associate at the counter."

He waved her over to me. I rolled my eyes. Associate?

"So how is business?" Tammy asked excitedly.

"Booming!" Dev rubbed his hands together gleefully.

I waited as Mrs. Fourteenth Ohio filled out her shipping information and wrote a check, then placed it with the others in our lockbox.

"Knew it!" Tammy clapped, bouncing up and down on her heels. "Y'all are the talk of Sutlers' Row. Buzz has been building, spreadin' all the way to the outskirts of the Union camp. Ran into a lady all the way from *Maine* who was headed to you!"

"Genius!" Dev shrieked. "I am a genius!"

"I knew you were!" she said, and patted his back.

I thanked Mrs. Fourteenth Ohio for her purchase and sent her on her way, making sure I carefully filed her shipping info with the burgeoning list of orders Dev would have to fill.

"What now? Who's next? Step right up!" Dev addressed the emptying row of tents. "I will sew you a dream! Spin straw into gold! The angels will weep tears of joy at your beauty!"

Dev had indeed gotten coffee from the Union troops this morning, and I think the sudden influx of caffeine into his system may have been too much for him.

"Aw, hon, take a break." Tammy patted his arm. "Y'all have to, anyway. Everythin' shuts down for the battle, and it's just about that time."

"*Everything* shuts down?" Dev turned to me, wide-eyed. "The genius wants some kettle corn."

"Well, I think y'all sure deserve some kettle corn!" Tammy squeezed him tightly.

"Libbeeee," Dev whined, "will you get me some kettle corn? I'd go myself, only I'm just . . . so . . . *tired.*" He wilted dramatically into Tammy's arms.

"Why you poor thing." Tammy felt his forehead to see if he had a fever and clucked sympathetically. "He's all tuckered out. Here, Libby," Tammy said, reaching into the small crocheted reticule dangling around her wrist and extracting a bill. "Get him some kettle corn, and some for you, and some for Beau, if y'all don't mind findin' him before the battle."

"I don't mind." I took the money and left, marching down the lane toward the food sutlers. "Don't mind at all," I muttered again, once they were out of earshot. "Sure, I'll get you your kettle corn. Don't mind at all." I mean, seriously. What was I, his personal assistant? His kettle corn waitress? Ridiculous.

It was funny. Most of the soldiers placed so much emphasis on period authenticity, but the minute the camp was open to the public, it was crawling with tourists dripping in grease from Indian fry bread and cracking open Cokes. I mean, the public couldn't step onto the battlefield, but they mingled in and out among the tents, talking to the soldiers. Which was, I suppose, the point, but it certainly looked strange. A family in matching Mickey Mouse T-shirts and fanny packs was deep in conversation with a particularly grimy Confederate soldier. Certainly something I never thought I'd see.

Seized with a sudden curiosity, I turned out of Sutlers' Row and clambered up the hill toward the lone, shiny white tent. It did indeed say "Dixie Acres" in glittery peach script and, strangely enough, was perched just outside the border of the reenactment. I lifted up the tent flap, pushed my way in, and was greeted by a frigid blast of cold air. Was this tent *air-conditioned?* I didn't even know that was possible!

"Hi, there!" a male voice boomed, over a Muzak version of "Tara's Theme." It was the man in the starched suit who'd been arguing with Cody. He smiled, displaying more white teeth than I thought was possible to fit inside a human mouth. "For chrissakes, Cheyenne, get up!" he hissed through his seemingly endless row of clenched teeth.

A blond woman in a peach sateen Southern belle costume

and a Mrs. America sash, whom I hadn't noticed before, rocketed out of a folding chair in the corner of the room, mulishly clutching a Diet Coke.

"You seem a little young to be looking for some real estate," the man said, chuckling. "Your daddy around, sugar?"

"No, he's in Minnesota," I replied, focusing on the center of the room. Atop a table stood a miniature housing development, chock-full of replicas of plantation homes. A thousand tiny Taras all smooshed together.

"That's awfully far away. Well, next time you see him, why don't you give him one of these." He waited a minute, smiling, before growling, "Cheyenne!"

The Southern belle stepped forward and handed me a brochure. I glanced at the cover and read:

> Bring the past into the present . . . with Dixie Acres!
> All the glory of the Old South with all the comforts of today.

I shuddered involuntarily—how tacky—before folding it up and sticking it down my dress for perusal at a later time. Luckily, I was able to beat a hasty retreat as the man had started berating the Southern belle for spilling Diet Coke on something. After the strangeness of the tent, it was almost a relief to be back in the stifling heat, and I hurried down the hill to Sutlers' Row.

Just past Old Doc Bell's Wizard Elixir (I had no idea what was in those green bottles, but I wasn't adventurous enough to find out), I arrived at the little red kettle corn tent and purchased an eighteen-inch bag. Plastic. Hmm . . . I probably shouldn't bring that into the encampment. Popcorn would be okay, though. I mean, even if popcorn didn't become extremely popular until the 1890s, after the invention of the first popcorn machine, a 1,000-year-old popped kernel had been found in southwestern Utah. In the sixteenth century Cortés reported that the Aztecs enjoyed popcorn, seventeenth-century French fur traders said the same of the Iroquois, and popcorn may even have been an hors d'oeuvre at the first Thanksgiving, as Native Americans often brought it as a snack during meetings with early English colonists. So even if it wasn't typical Confederate fare, technically it wasn't historically inaccurate. The plastic bag, not so much.

"I mean, really, they needed me." Dev and Tammy were still talking in the tent when I returned. "These women are just beyond tragic!"

"Honey, I know, I know." Tammy shook her head.

Dev was actually right. Not everyone took accuracy as seriously as the Fifteenth Alabama, and many of the women looked like they had purchased Southern belle costumes at Party City or were recycling old prom dresses. Of course, some of them looked absolutely flawless, but there were more than a few who needed Dev's help.

"These women needed me," he said, "and at their darkest hour of need, I arrived."

"Here ya go." I dropped the popcorn on the table. "Now, can I get you anything else, sir? Coffee? Evian? Massage?"

"Maybe later." Dev chose to ignore my sarcasm and opened the popcorn. "Delicious."

"Do you have anything I can put some popcorn in to take to Beau?" I asked.

"Oh, because it's plastic?" Tammy asked. I nodded. "Aren't you thoughtful! Just the sweetest thing, isn't she?"

"Most of the time." Dev rustled around and pulled out a handkerchief. "Here, put some in this. Not too much!" he cautioned anxiously.

I spread open the handkerchief. "LK?" There was a little pink monogram in one corner.

"I embroidered them for you. There's a whole stack." And that was Dev in a nutshell. Just when you thought he was being ridiculous, he'd go and do something amazing like that. I put a handful of kettle corn into the handkerchief and tied it up.

"Twenty minutes to battle!" blared out over the PA system.

"Run, doll!" Tammy shooed me out of the tent. "They muster at fifteen."

We were all the way on the Confederate end of Sutlers' Row, so it was only a quick run down the hill to the encampment. Once I was there, however, I had no idea where to go. All of the tents were indistinguishable, and they stretched on seemingly forever. I headed down one row of tents, as all around me Confederate men put on their jackets, exited their tents, and started making their way toward the battlefield.

"Where's the fire, sweetheart?" one called after me as I raced by, picking up speed the longer I went without seeing any familiar tents. "What's your rush, doll? We've got more'n fifteen minutes!" another called.

Another row of tents—and nothing.

"Who're you lookin' for, darlin'?" An old man shrugging on a long officer's coat called to me as I rounded the edge of one row of tents.

"The Fifteenth Alabama," I yelled back.

"Two rows down, all the way on the other side. Should be about to muster, though."

"Thank you!"

I took off in the direction he'd indicated. By the time I spotted the top of a head with a familiar auburn tint to it, the camp was abuzz with activity, and the grassy lanes formed by the makeshift tent village were swarming with men.

"Beau!" I called. In the sea of butternut browns and shades of gray, the russet-colored blur stopped and turned. Since I was dressed all in white and about a head shorter than everyone else, I was pretty easy to spot. Beau made his way over to me.

"Libby, what the hell are you doin' out here?" He grabbed my arm, steadying me, to keep me from being swept away on the Rebel tide. "We're startin' to line up. It's almost time for the battle to begin."

As if on cue, the fife and drums on the edge of the battlefield burst into a spirited rendition of "Dixie."

"Oh, I'm sorry, I didn't mean to—I brought you this, I—Here . . ." I held out the little white bundle.

He took it, perplexed, and peeled back a corner of the handkerchief. "Popcorn?" A look of disbelief passed over his face. "Popcorn?" he repeated again, dumbstruck. Beau looked up at me and grinned. "You ran all the way the hell out here, practically in the middle of battle, to bring me popcorn?"

"It's kettle corn," I replied, somewhat defensively.

Beau threw back his head and laughed. "Kettle corn." He popped several kernels in his mouth. "Delicious." He swallowed and tossed in another handful. "I never had anyone bring me a battle snack before. You got a juice box hidden up your shimmy too?"

"Next time," I promised, grinning.

BOOM! I turned toward the noise. On the Union side of the field, a cloud of smoke arose from a cannon way in the distance.

"Hell, that'll be fifteen. Artillery's doin' a safety check," Beau said, indicating the spot in the field where the cannon smoke lingered.

Sure enough, the loudspeaker boomed, "Fifteen minutes to battle! Troops, report to your officers and line up for inspection!"

Goodness! It was hard not to get swept up in the spirit of things. My heart was pounding in its corseted prison, what with all the excitement, and men rushing around, and horses pawing at the grass.

"Well . . ." I turned to Beau. I had no idea what to say in this situation. *Have fun? Good luck? Break a leg?* Nothing seemed right.

"Shoot, do you need your handkerchief back?" He hadn't quite finished the kettle corn.

"No, you keep it," I said. "For, um, luck."

Beau nodded, smiled, and ate the last handful of popcorn. Then he tucked the handkerchief into the inside pocket of his jacket. "Kiss for good luck?" He turned his cheek to me. On the cheek, right? There was no harm in that, surely. You kissed elderly relatives there. I reached up on my tiptoes and deposited a swift peck on his cheek. A shadow of stubble scratched against my lips in a manner not altogether unpleasant. "Now I can die a happy man," he said with a grin.

"No, don't say that!" I gasped. "You're not going to die! I'm sure you'll come back just fine." It took me a minute to remember that it was all pretend. Out here, with the smoke and the fires and the endless sea of troops, it all just seemed so real.

"Nope, my number's up." He readjusted the rifle hanging over his back. "Each battle is an exact re-creation of the actual one durin' the Civil War, and we were pretty much slaughtered here. Tannehill was one of the main sources of Confederate iron durin' the war, and the Eighth Iowa Cavalry damn near burned it to the ground. I'm marchin' out to my death, but I'll go with a smile on my face." Something over my head caught Beau's attention. "My line's formin' up." He nodded toward the field. "But I go off to fight with a handkerchief in my pocket from the prettiest Yankee playin' Rebel I've ever seen."

Before I could quite figure out what to say to that, he'd left to join his regiment. All the men had emptied out of the camp to line up, so I ran as quickly as I could back to the civilian side. We were separated from the battle by a thin white rope that ran the length of the designated field, winding its way through a stretch of woods in the state park. Dev, holding a lace parasol, waved me over impatiently.

"Um, hello, took you long enough! Here"—he shoved the parasol in my face. "What did I tell you about protecting your porcelain complexion? Did you have to run all over Alabama without a hat? Kettle corn?" He held out the bag.

"Thanks." I took a few pieces and munched them nervously. That whole exchange had left me slightly uncomfortable, afraid that I was getting too close to crossing some sort of line. That hadn't been too flirtatious, right? I mean, not really. It was all just pretend. Because I had a completely awesome boyfriend in Boston, and Beau was just a friend whom I had kissed on the cheek before he headed off to die. I mean, that's what friends are for, right?

"Look at this," Dev said, holding up a schedule in front of my nose. He jabbed a finger somewhere near the bottom.

"'Chirping Chicken Chase, courtesy of the Greater Tuscaloosa Grange Fair'?" I asked, puzzled. That didn't really seem like Dev's scene.

"No, no, below that," he said, rolling his eyes. "Eight p.m. Ball!"

"Ball?!"

"Ball!" Dev confirmed. "Tammy told me all about it. Don't worry, this one's not super formal—just dancing outside under a big tent on the battlefield. We'll still be the best-dressed ones there though, obvi. But we'll wait till we hit this super-fancy plantation to pull out the big guns—apparently once we're done with North Carolina and start marching back from the sea, there's a big-deal ball on our way back. *Everyone* who's anyone goes. Southerners, Northerners, doesn't matter. There's no blue and gray when it's all glitter and gold. Très swank."

"We're going all the way to North Carolina?" I asked, surprised.

"We've done 'Bama, baby. There's a whole South to see." He gestured grandly. "Talked to Tammy about the hygiene sitch, p to the s. Trucker showers."

"That sounds dirtier than not showering," I said skeptically.

"No, really, she assured me it's fine. Truck stops have showers. Clean and wholesome. All yours for seven bucks. We'll stop at one the next time we hit the road. Come on, Libs." He shrugged, eyeing my dubious look. "If Tammy Anderson has no problem taking a trucker shower, I'm sure it's more than good enough for you and me."

Dev pulled an old-fashioned telescope out of his coat and held it to his eye.

"Did you swipe that from Jack Sparrow?" I quipped. I mean, really, he looked like a Confederate pirate. "What on earth are you doing?"

"Trying to spot the hotties," he said, squinting toward the Union troops. "I swapped a hat for it. This way, I figure I'll have a tactical advantage. I'll hit that ball one step ahead."

"Seriously?" I rolled my eyes. "Can you even see—"

"Ladies and gentlemen!" a voice boomed over the field. "Welcome to the Battle of Tannehill! Let the fighting . . . begin!"

Over on the Union side, a bugle call spurred the troops into action. The Confederates collectively let out a bloodcurdling Rebel yell and ran to meet them in the middle.

Funnily enough, the loudspeaker continued to narrate as the battle progressed, like it was some kind of sporting event.

"And here comes the cavalry!" the PA system announced. "The Eighth Iowa sweeps through, cutting off the Confederates on their left flank."

Sure enough, horses thundered past from both sides, and cannons exploded across the field, every step of the way narrated by the announcer. Once the cavalry swept through, they circled back, waiting behind the lines of men hidden behind embankments or moving slowly forward in long, rigid lines.

"Um, if this is war," Dev shouted over the cannons, "why is it so effin' boring?"

I hated to admit it, but he was sort of right. Warfare was

surprisingly . . . slow. Lines of men would shoot, reload, and advance a few feet, before repeating the whole process. Except for the men on horseback circling the battle, they moved at an almost glacial pace.

Most of the Confederates had hunkered down behind earthen ramifications they'd built earlier, shooting over the tops of the little walls. The only real spot of excitement came when one Confederate decided to desert, and one of his fellow soldiers turned around and shot him in the face.

"Harsh!" Dev said, aghast. "Way harsh."

"Dev, you know they're firing blanks, right?" I said.

I watched the progression of another soldier as he crawled, wounded, slowly down the length of the entire field, and somehow managed to make it back to his troop.

Dev peered through the telescope. "Oh, I think I found Beau."

"What? Where?" I clutched his sleeve. "Is he still alive?"

"No, he was killed by a puff of smoke in the land of make-believe. Yes, he's still alive." Dev pointed toward the embankment closest to us. "But he's still fighting, if that's what you meant."

I followed his arm, and there was Beau, behind the little earth mound, reloading. Slowly, soldiers fell around him, as the announcer spoke glowingly of the tide turning to Union victory. And then, after just another crack of shots in an endless series, Beau shuddered, slumped, and was still. I screamed and buried my face in Dev's jacket.

"Oh, drama queen, get over yourself," he said, as he shook me off. "If you want to mourn anything, mourn the fact that we still have another hour to go of watching this snooze-fest."

"Sorry, sorry," I apologized, extricating myself. "It just looked so . . . real."

"Um, real?" Dev pointed at a teenage girl with green nail polish in a ragtag Confederate uniform who had died and then sat up to watch the rest of the battle.

"Okay, maybe not all of it."

The battle dragged on for a full two hours, and as we were standing there in the hot sun, it felt even longer. Eventually, however, nearly all of the Confederates lay dead, Dev had spotted all of the attractive men, and the announcer was proclaiming it a decisive Union victory.

"Well, that took long enough," Dev said, as he collapsed his telescope. "Back to business."

Dev practically dragged me away up to our tent on Sutlers' Row, the Rodeo Drive of the reenactment, where we continued to custom-fit couture for the masses. Except for a quick dinner break when I went to buy us some delicious, if not particularly historically accurate, hot dogs, we were busy right up until the end of the business day, when everyone took off to watch the Chirping Chicken Chase. I was all set to chase the chickens, but Dev insisted we itemize receipts instead. Which was probably a smart idea, but I kind of wanted to see the chickens.

Between finishing the business day, packing up everything, and getting ready for the ball, we were busy until eight o'clock, because Dev's idea of "casual" ball wear involved a greenish-blue shot-silk gown for me and a white suit with matching shot-silk waistcoat for him.

As Dev had predicted, we were the best-dressed ones there. It was really beautiful under the tent. It definitely wasn't fancy, with rough wooden benches at the edges of the muslin tent stretching down the length of the field, but beautiful nonetheless, lanterns twinkling from the crossbeams of the sloping ceiling. A band played merrily in one corner, and in front of them, a dancing master called out the steps. It sounded like a square dance: "Right hand around, left hand around, forward and back, ladies curtsy." Two long rows of couples stood facing each other, skipping and twirling around in sync.

"Punch bowl, punch bowl, punch bowl," Dev muttered distractedly. "Bingo!"

"Wait a minute." I grabbed his arm as he started off. "Don't just leave me here—I don't know anyone."

"Sure you do."

I turned. Beau was standing behind me.

"You're alive!" I cried, and flung my arms around his middle.

"Hell yeah, I'm alive. I never miss a reel," he said, and chuckled.

"Speaking of reels, I'm gonna try to reel me in a man in uniform." Dev pointed toward the punch bowl, where a boy in blue with ridiculously long eyelashes was sipping a glass, looking around the dance floor. "I'll let you two joyously reunite. Toodles."

He scooted off, sidling through the rows of couples.

"So here you are, back from the dead," I said, as the band finished a song and the rows of couples clapped.

"Alive and kickin'." Beau nodded. "An' speakin' of kickin', how 'bout a dance?"

"Oh, I don't know any of these dances," I hemmed and hawed.

"Libby, there's a man out front callin' out the steps. You don't have to know anythin'. They tell you what to do."

"Well, true." That was a good point. But was it okay to dance with him? I mean, I had a boyfriend. Probably Garrett wouldn't mind. It was just a dance. But it's not like Beau was Dev. Beau was single, straight, and had said I was pretty . . .

"Fine, you want to do this the right way?" Beau held out his hand. "Accordin' to *Beadle's Dime Book of Practical Etiquette,* the words 'Will you honor me with your hand?' are used more nowadays. Nowadays 1860, that is." The band started tuning up for the next song. "So, Libby, will you honor me with your hand?" He looked down at me, expectantly, and I looked at his hand. "Sounds like a reel." He cocked his head toward the band. "Real easy. Bad pun intended." He smiled.

I took his hand. His grin widened, and he led me onto the floor, where we joined the line of couples. Beau was right; it turned out to be not that hard to follow. I mean, the dance master told you exactly what to do. I only went the wrong way, like, twice.

"You're such a good dancer!" I exclaimed, surprised. He really was.

"Well, I've been doin' this forever. Most reenactments have dances," Beau said. He spun me effortlessly as we changed partners. I mean, I was following along okay, but I certainly wasn't good. Beau, however, steered me safely through the line and almost managed to make me look like I knew what I was doing.

It was more fun than I'd had in a long time. I could have reeled and quadrilled all night long, and time flew by.

"And now," the dancing master said, interrupting the proceedings after we'd been dancing for some time. "I know much of small-town America is scandalized by these new, modern 'round dances,' but here in Tuscaloosa, we're a little more forward-thinking."

Everyone chuckled. Someone yelled out, "Keep that trash for the romping female animals of Yankee land! Our real Southern ladies won't do it!"

"Like hell we won't!" a woman yelled back, causing a raucous outburst of laughter.

"'Round dances'?" I whispered.

"Waltz, polka. Things like that where the couples dance close together, not all in a line. People were still scandalized by that down here durin' the war, even though it was already old news back in Europe and in the bigger cities up north," Beau explained.

"The ladies have spoken!" the dancing master shouted out. "Gents, choose your ladies for the waltz."

Beau held out his hand.

"Oh, um, I don't know how to waltz. And I'm pretty sure the dancing master won't tell us how to do it."

"You don't know how to waltz?" He furrowed his brow. "How is that possible?"

"There's not a lot of waltzing going on in St. Paul," I said, shrugging.

"Well, I'll have to teach you before the big ball of the season, up at this old restored plantation in a few weeks." His hand was still out. "But for now, just try to follow along."

"I'm really not that coordinated, and I don't know how, and I don't think I can—"

Beau ignored my protests and pulled me into him, so we

were standing in a waltz position. It was funny—by modern dancing standards, we weren't close at all, but he felt so uncomfortably near that my heart was starting to pound.

"AAAAAAAAAAAAAAAAAAA!!!!!!!!!!!!!!!"

A bloodcurdling shriek ripped through the party, causing the tuning fiddle to break off abruptly. A little drummer boy, probably about ten years old and screaming bloody murder, ran straight into my skirts, hiding his face.

"I wanna g-go home," he sobbed, hiccupping. "I wanna go home!"

"Hey," I said, as I knelt down. "Are you okay? What's going on?"

"Jackie?" Beau asked. "Is that you?"

Everyone at the ball had stopped whatever they were doing and was staring at us.

"G-g-ghost," he stuttered. "I saw her. Oh, I wanna go home," he wailed.

"Okay, who are you here with?" I asked, rubbing his back soothingly. "I'll help you find your family, okay?"

"I'm with the Fif-fifteenth Alabama." He hiccupped again. Ah, that explained it—he must have run straight for the nearest thing to a mom in the Fifteenth Alabama. And as I was the only girl, that would be me. "You're Cody's girlfriend, right?"

I shot Beau a look.

"This is Jackson." Beau knelt down next to us. "He's with the Boy Scout troop that's marching with us."

"Don't touch me!" Jackson shrieked, shoving Beau away and trying to burrow into my neck. "She's coming for you!"

"Who's coming? What's going on?" I was so completely lost.

"Jackson." Captain Cauldwell had pushed his way over to

join us. "Why don't you tell me what's going on, son? Wanna show me what scared you?"

Jackson straightened and nodded, silent tears still glistening on his cheeks. He took my hand, and together we led Captain Cauldwell out of the tent. Beau grabbed a lantern and trailed a few paces behind. Most of the dancers had left the ball and were following us.

Jackson led us deeper into the woods. He bypassed an oddly rustling bush.

"OMG, do you think they heard us?" Dev popped out of the bush, holding hands with the Union soldier with beautiful giraffe eyelashes. I shook my head and motioned for him to follow. They did, swelling the strange lantern-bearing mob of Civil War dancers by two more.

Jackson stopped in a clearing and pointed to a dirty, tattered muslin tarp. I gasped and covered his eyes. Something was written on it, in dripping, red-brown letters, and from the dead chicken lying nearby, I feared it was written in blood. I turned Jackson away from the Chirping Chicken Chase casualty and tried not to shake.

"What does it say?" I whispered.

From behind me, Beau held up his lantern and read, in the flickering shadows, "Anderson."

chapter four

I'd insisted that Beau leave Willie stationed outside Jackson's tent, but he'd done a terrible job as a guard dog—Jackson and his tentmate had seen the shadow of the ghost again during the night and were now both insisting on leaving immediately. Willie was still sleeping soundly when I crept past him the next morning to sneak into the woods so I could call Garrett. He wasn't going to believe this.

"Yeah, that's right." I heard a voice speaking low in the woods. Sounded like someone had already beaten me to the secret cell phone spot. "Just the one *s*."

Cody was standing in the woods, furtively covering his cell phone with his hand.

"What are you doing, young man?" I marched straight up to him, like I was a hall monitor or something, about to confiscate his phone.

"Yeah, that's right. Gotta go, man, bye." He hurriedly finished and snapped the phone shut, then stuffed it into the back pocket of his brown wool pants.

"Mmm-hmmm?" I folded my arms as he looked guiltily up at me. "So?" I tapped my foot.

"What?" He folded his arms too. "What do you want from me? And what all were you doin' out here, anyway?" he added suspiciously.

"I was, uh, on a walk," I said defensively. "I came out for some fresh air."

"You live in a tent. It doesn't have walls. Don't tell me that's not enough fresh air for you."

I glared. "Seriously. Who were you talking to? What are you doing?" It was weird the way he'd been covering up his phone. It seemed fishy.

"Just . . . just tellin' my friends at home. About the ghost."

I arched an eyebrow.

"Well, I had to tell them about somethin'. I'm havin' about the lamest summer ever, so at least this is sorta interestin'." He kicked a rock with the sole of his boot.

"What are you talking about?" I asked, genuinely surprised. "This summer is awesome! You must be having lots of fun. I know I am."

"Um, no." We started making our way back to camp. "Being a Boy Scout is lame as crap already; then add to that all these weirdo history freaks, and it's even worse. Normal people don't spend their summers runnin' around in itchy wool pants in a hundred-degree heat, pretendin' to shoot at each other and fallin' over, fakin' dead. It's weird."

"Well, sure, it's unusual, but doing stuff that's different is cool. Who wants to be normal, anyway, right? That's kind of lame in its own way, you know. Just following the pack." Maybe I could still win him over, somehow get him to see that history, contrary to popular disgruntled teen belief, was actually awesome.

"I'd never be here if my stupid mom didn't make me, so she could spend the summer with her new boyfriend," he complained. "All my friends are back home in Montgomery, hangin' out at the mall, doing cool shit at the skate park, drinkin' Slurpees. Apparently it's so hot there, Melissa Cooper's been wearin' shorts so short you can see part of her butt," he added wistfully. "And she was a runner-up in Miss Alabama's Outstanding Teen Pageant. And believe you me, she is outstanding."

"Um, as fun as that sounds," I said, swallowing uncomfortably, "you're having the kind of experience here that so few people have. You're really lucky. This is a once-in-a-lifetime opportunity, and—"

"And I'm stuck here all summer"—Cody continued talking over me—"and the only decent-looking girl is a stuck-up, frigid Yankee prude!"

"What!" I gasped. "I am not a prude! Or frigid. Or stuck-up. And there's nothing wrong with Yankees!"

"Prove it." Cody stopped in his tracks.

"What?"

"Yeah. Prove it. Show me how much fun you are." He closed his eyes and puckered his lips. This was getting ridiculous.

"Cody." I clapped my hands in front of his face, and, startled, he opened his eyes. "Stop. You have to stop. Seriously. I will have you . . . court-martialed if you keep this up." I mean, I didn't really know if I could court-martial him, but it sounded like an appropriate military threat.

"Why?" he mumbled mutinously.

"One, you're way too young for me; two, with this kind of attitude, I wouldn't date you even if you were nineteen; and, three, I have a boyfriend."

"Aw, not Corporal Lame-ass Anderson?" He shoved his hands in his pockets and continued shuffling back toward camp. "Even after I warned you that boy was cursed? Even now that you've seen, firsthand, the kind of seriously evil shit he's drawin' down on all of us? You can't still wanna get mixed up with that crazy, dark voodoo-zombie shit."

"What? No," I said, surprised. "Corporal Anderson and I aren't involved. At all. I have a boyfriend in Boston. And I don't believe in 'crazy, dark voodoo-zombie shit,' anyway."

"What, you got a boyfriend way back up north?" He shook his head. "That don't even count. Those kinds of things don't hold up across state lines or time zones. It's part of international law," he said seriously. "Don't even think about that. Think about what's here. Alabama is for lovers, baby."

"That's Virginia," I said, grabbing him by the ear.

"Ow, Libby, ow!" he yelled.

"We're done here." I dragged Cody back to camp by his ear, listening to him shriek all the way. I deposited him roughly outside the tent where Randall was marshaling up the Boy Scouts. "Keep track of this," I said, nodding to Randall, who fixed Cody with an especially pinch-faced look, narrowing his eyes until they resembled snake-like slits. Randall's troops were now down to only six, as Jackson and his tentmate were waiting in the parking lot for their moms to pick them up. The rest of them would be continuing on with us to Georgia, on the Atlanta campaign, but it felt somewhat ominous to have our number reduced by two.

Captain Cauldwell ordered the men to break down camp and to table any discussion of the "situation" until we made camp in Georgia. Dev and I, helpful as always, waited in the parking lot until the deserting Boy Scouts had been dispatched, the tents broken down, and Beau was ready to drive us to Georgia.

"I feel terrible," Beau murmured once we were on our way.

"Don't you dare," I said. "Don't you dare feel bad. It wasn't your fault! You had nothing to do with this."

"I know, but still . . . I feel terrible." He shook his head. "It was my name written in blood on that sheet. I can't help but feel partly responsible. Those poor kids, bein' so scared that they left for home, callin' their mamas, cryin' . . . I just feel awful."

"How do you think I feel?" Dev demanded. "I just bid adieu to the love of my life!"

"Oh, the Union soldier?" I asked. He nodded and looked tragically out the window, like he was on a soap opera. Dev typically fell in love twenty times a month, so I was well versed in how to help him get over it quickly.

"'Once upon a time, I was falling in love,'" I sang softly.

"'Now I'm only falling apart,'" Dev whispered dramatically.

"'There's nothing I can do,'" I sang, and then he joined me for "'a total eclipse of the heart.'"

Thankfully, Beau chose to ignore us instead of asking if we were crazy. Sometimes the best way to help Dev deal with his current drama was just to let him wallow in it for a bit.

After a brief but much-appreciated visit to a truck stop shower, where I discovered that trucker showers were not gross at all, we hit the road. Beau was uncharacteristically glum, and we sat in a morose silence punctuated only by the light rustle of Dev's breathing as he snored softly and the raspy sound of Willie panting.

Since no one in the truck seemed predisposed to entertain me, I unfolded the Dixie Acres brochure I'd set aside while packing up last night. I grimaced slightly at the glossy picture of a mini Tara framed by magnolia blossoms, before opening the brochure and reading:

> Own your very own piece of history! Luxury gated communities and upscale condominiums located in the heart of Dixie . . . on actual Civil War battlefields!

Wait a minute. That couldn't be right. You couldn't build anything on a battlefield . . . could you?

"Hey, Beau?" I asked tentatively. "Are Civil War battlefields protected? Like by the National Register of Historic Places or something?"

"Some are, but some aren't, unfortunately," he answered. "The big ones—Gettysburg, Antietam, et cetera—they're all fine. But the smaller ones, if they don't have any kind of protection program or public ownership, can be in danger from modern construction. Especially if they haven't been included in historic resource inventories, which if the local government thinks it just looks like a field, they usually aren't. So you lose some of the smaller ones. Hell, the Confederate trenches at Port Hudson got turned into a landfill, a highway runs through Kennesaw, and Prairie Grove is covered in poultry sheds. There was almost a shopping mall built on Manassas, for chrissakes." Beau fell silent again, looking even unhappier than before.

Wow. I felt almost sick to my stomach. So it *was* possible that Dixie Acres could turn some of these historic sites into housing developments. I frowned at the picture inside, which showed a blond woman serving iced tea to a group of children on a small front porch, and read on:

> Coming soon to a southern-fried state near you—Alabama, Georgia, Tennessee, and the Carolinas. Meet you under the magnolia blossoms!

Had they already purchased the land? In five different states? How had no one stopped them? Everywhere I went there were hundreds of Civil War buffs who you'd think would be desperate to stop this—to raise money to protect the battlefields, to do *something*. I resolved to show the brochure to Beau when he was in a better mood. And maybe to Captain Cauldwell, too.

The Battle of Atlanta wasn't actually taking place in Atlanta, but a few miles south in a little town called Hampton. The Nash Farm Battlefield was enormous, and with good reason. Once we arrived at the Registration Building, a sprawling white farmhouse in the heart of the field, we learned that there were more than twelve hundred reenactors enlisted. The little cash register in Dev's head rang audibly.

It was a beautiful stretch of soft green rolling hills, low rambling bushes, and flowering trees, interrupted only by earthenware trenches already dug in preparation for the battle. Sutlers' Row was up by the Registration Building, facing kitty-corner to a little living history village with a schoolhouse, an "Activity Barn," and a few other farmhouses. The men helped us set up our tent and then marched off to the Confederate camp, which was so far away on the other end of the field, it was barely visible. Dev and I settled down for a quiet night. I had thought, then, that maybe Captain Cauldwell had decided to just let sleeping ghosts lie.

They certainly hadn't decided to let sleeping couturiers lie. We were awoken by an ear-splitting blast.

"What . . . the hell . . . is that," Dev uttered, sitting up in bed.

"I think it's a bugle." I pulled my pillow over my head.

"Why is it so loud?" Dev clapped his hands over his ears. "I thought we could sleep in today! The camp's not open to the public; most of the other units aren't even here yet! MAKE IT STOP!"

It really was loud. Very, very loud.

"*You* make it stop!" I shouted back. "Go see what it is!"

"You go!"

"I'm in my underwear!"

"So am I!"

"But mine is see-through, and I'm a lady!"

"You're closer!"

"FINE!" I couldn't take it anymore. The noise was driving me insane. Modesty be damned. I stuck my head out of the tent. "WHAT?!"

Randall was standing outside our tent, puffing on a little brass bugle, red in the face. He broke off abruptly. "Meeting in fifteen at the schoolhouse for the whole unit. Captain Cauldwell says that includes you two."

He started bugling again. Dev, groggy, staggered in behind me, stuck his arm out of the tent, and covered the end of the horn with his hand.

"Yeah, no," Dev said. "We're done here. On your way, little boy."

Looking slightly defeated, Randall dragged himself back to the camp.

"Fifteen? As in fifteen minutes?" I asked. Dev was already back in bed. "No, no, no sleeping." I pulled him out by the ankles. "We have to go."

"I . . . don't . . . wanna." He clung to his pillow stubbornly, but I managed to wrestle him out of his cot. There wasn't a lot to hold on to, it being a tent and all.

Grudgingly, Dev pulled on a pair of purplish plaid plain-cut summer trousers, fastened his suspenders over a white bib-front shirt, and tied on a large floppy floral neckerchief at a rakish angle, sort of like a Pink Lady from *Grease.* By the time I'd been wrangled into a puff-sleeved, boat-necked lavender gingham and pink-flowered number, we were nearly late. Even with a time crunch, we looked fabulous. Also, I noted with some dismay, we matched. Before we scrambled out of the tent, I grabbed my Dixie Acres brochure. Just in case.

Everyone else was already seated in the schoolhouse when we crept into the back, trying to be unobtrusive, which was not so easy to do in lavender. The room did a collective double take at our pastel synchronicity before turning their attention back to Captain Cauldwell, who was standing by a chalkboard at the front of the room.

"Ahem." Captain Cauldwell cleared his throat, his mustache bristling.

"Sorry!" Dev whispered loudly as we slid into the last row of benches in the one-room schoolhouse. Beau turned around from the front row and winked.

It was a very small schoolhouse, with only four rows of benches three deep, and room for only two people on each.

However, there were only fifteen enlisted men in the Fifteenth Alabama—it always felt like more, because we were usually in the midst of masses of Confederate camps, but on our own, there were fifteen soldiers, six Boy Scouts, and two pastel-plaid civilians.

"I had hoped not to make an issue out of this," Captain Cauldwell said, frowning. "However . . ." He cleared his throat again and closed his eyes. "Lieutenant, if you would."

A man in the front row stood up, a stack of newspapers under his arm. He dropped the first one on the wooden lectern at the front of the room.

"Tuscaloosa News," Captain Cauldwell announced. *"Mobile Press-Register."* Another hit the lectern. *"Huntsville Times."* Another. *"Birmingham News."* Another. "The four biggest papers in Alabama. And here's the real kicker, the *Atlanta Journal-Constitution.*" All of the papers were stacked on the table. "Biggest newspaper south of D.C. And we weren't even in Georgia!" He scratched his head. "We weren't even in Georgia," he repeated, bewildered. "Somebody mind tellin' me how that happened?"

"How what happened, Captain?" one of the men asked.

"How every single one of these papers has an article on that damn ghost stalking our boys," he muttered blackly. A low murmur started gathering steam around the room. "How I've got mothers callin' me on my emergency cell—which I ain't even supposed to be usin'—frantic, askin' me what kind of operation I'm runnin' here, askin' me if this is my idea of a joke, askin' me if I think this is funny." The murmurings increased. "Quiet!" Captain Cauldwell barked, and the room went instantly silent.

"Now, this ain't my idea of a joke," Captain Cauldwell continued, "but if one of you boys pulled a prank that got a little out of hand, I'd sure appreciate it if you spoke up, before things get even more out of hand."

"What kind of sick crazy bastard murders an innocent chicken for a prank?!" I whispered to Dev.

"You think that chicken was murdered?" Dev whispered back. "You suspect . . . fowl play?"

"Well, yeah. Chickens don't bleed to death from natural causes."

"A murder most . . . fowl?" He giggled. "Get it? Fowl? Foul?"

"Har-har-har," I said sarcastically. "Puns are not your strong suit."

"SHHH!" Randall turned around and shushed us from the front of the room. Sheesh. We weren't being *that* loud.

Captain Cauldwell was still talking. "The brave young soldiers of Boy Scout Troop 72 are just as much a part of this unit as any of you enlisted men, and I don't like to lose a single soldier. And if this ghost nonsense keeps up, I don't know how many men we'll lose. We lost two good men yesterday, and we'll be down another today, as Private Hennessy's mama just informed me she ain't lettin' him stay here."

"I can stay. I ain't scared," one of the Boy Scouts, presumably Private Hennessy, piped up.

"I know, son, but your mama said pack, and that's an order." Captain Cauldwell sighed with resignation. The Boy Scouts really were dropping out at an alarming rate. "She'll be here to pick you up before nightfall. And in addition, we all look pretty damn near ridiculous in these papers, and I hate lookin' like a fool. So I'm gonna ask, one more time, with total amnesty for the perpetrators if y'all come clean right now: Were any of you behind this?"

Silence.

"I think it's the Yanks, tryin' to rattle us!" one of the men eventually suggested.

"Or the Fourteenth Alabama Hilliby True Blues! They're always tryin' to get our goat," another one said.

"Naw, definitely Yanks! Prob'ly those bastards from Ohio!" said another.

"Anyone from Pennsylvania! They're always angry!"

"Don't count out the Fifth Iowa Cavalry!"

"I think it's bad voodoo! Like in *Midnight in the Garden of Good and Evil*!" Dev chimed in. I tried to shush him. "Or a dark lady! Like the Cher song! 'Dark Lady played black magic till the clock struck on the twelve'—urgh!" I elbowed him in the ribs.

"It's the ghost of Anne Mitchell, out to wreak vengeance on Corporal Anderson!" Cody shouted. "She's real, and she's real angry! We all saw what was written on that sheet!"

"Private, you keep your voice down," Captain Cauldwell warned him. "Don't go spoutin' off that ridiculous nonsense. That's just a dumb story used to scare kids from Kentucky to Alabama. There's no such thing as ghosts, and there's nothin' wreakin' vengeance on Corporal Anderson or anybody else in this unit."

"You explain that to Jackson," Cody said, folding his arms defiantly. "Oh, wait, you can't. He's gone."

The men murmured among themselves, but no one seemed to have any pertinent information to volunteer.

"Anyone else?" Captain Cauldwell asked.

Almost surprising myself, I rose to my feet. Dev looked about as astonished as I felt. Every head in the room swiveled toward me.

"It's, um, not ghost related." I cleared my throat. "Has anyone heard of Dixie Acres? It's this housing development company, and they want to build gated communities on Civil War battlefields! On historic sites!"

"That sounds like a real shame, but if the battlefields are not federally protected, there's not a whole lot we can do," Captain Cauldwell said, shaking his head sadly.

"We have to try to do *something,*" I pressed on. "If it's not too late. Has anyone here heard of any battlefields being bought privately? For development?"

"I haven't," said Bill with the round glasses, and the rest of the men seemed to agree.

"So it's probably not too late!" I exclaimed. "Someone here would know if they'd bought the land—you can't keep something like that quiet. So we have to figure out how to stop them: maybe a petition, or raise money for a private trust, or try to get all of the battlefields listed on the National Register—"

"Libby," Captain Cauldwell interrupted me gently. "I understand that you're upset, but you also have to realize that you're new here and don't quite know the way things work. We're not a federal power, and we don't have the clout to protect every battlefield. And even if we did, the kind of action you're talkin' about would take years. Sounds like these Dixie Acres folks have stuff lined up already. We lose a little bit of land every year, and it's a damned shame, but that's just the way it is. I'm sorry, but I don't think there's anything we can do about it."

I slumped down dejectedly. Why wasn't anyone as upset about this as I was? Dev patted my hoop skirt comfortingly as Captain Cauldwell dismissed his men, and the meeting was adjourned.

We passed a quiet week at Nash Farm. The fighting didn't start until Friday, so it was only us and a handful of other hard-core reenacting regiments kicking around the sprawling property. Without any access to caffeine, Dev slept nearly twenty hours a day, much like a cat. Beau and I spent hours wandering around the farm, talking about history, and exploring the fields, and Beau attempted to teach me how to waltz. But that may have been a mission impossible. Dev woke up long enough every day to critique my technique and suggest that Beau would be much better off with him as a partner.

Once Friday rolled around, however, "quiet" was the last word to describe Nash Farm. Twelve hundred reenactors sounded like a lot, but once they were all actually here—running around, cleaning guns, lighting fires, tending pots, and making small explosions—they were more than I'd even imagined. The place was swarming with soldiers and echoing with chatter and laughter. All of this translated to even greater profits for Confederate Couture once the gates opened to the public at ten. We were busy moving merch straight through the Ninety-Seventh Regimental String Band's pre-battle prelude. Dev snoozed through the first day of the Battle of Jonesborough, his head lolling gently against my shoulder as Confederate Lieutenant General Hardee attacked Sherman's Union troops, who pushed him back easily, resulting in a Confederate retreat until the next day. It sort of took some of the suspense out of it when you already knew that this was the battle that would lead to the Confederate evacuation and the Union occupation of Atlanta, even if we wouldn't reach that conclusion until the end of the weekend. I mean, it was called "the last defense of Atlanta" right on the schedule. It was sort of like going to see *Titanic* and knowing that the ship was going to sink.

Dev disappeared right after the battle, leaving me to itemize the receipts, because I was "so much better at it." And Beau had survived the battle but had marched off with the rest of the men to the Confederate camp, way far away, so I was alone and sort of bored on Sutlers' Row. The sun set as I packed and stacked, until, under cover of darkness, Dev reappeared, sneaking stealthily among the shadows.

"Um, hello." I closed the account book, setting it by the lockbox. "What are you doing? Casing the joint?"

"Come here," Dev muttered. "I've got something to show you." He darted a nervous glance around. "In private."

"What, like a rash?" I asked nervously. "I would really appreciate it if this time you just went straight to the medical facilities and didn't ask me what I thought it was—"

"No, not a rash!" he yelled, then quieted instantly. "I can't tell you. Have to show you. In private."

"Okay, here, come on inside the sleeping tent. I was headed there, anyway."

"NO!" he objected. "No," he added in a whisper, clutching his jacket close. "We need to go away. Hide the valuables, and meet me outside the tent."

"Um, okay." This was weird behavior, even for Dev. Had

he acquired an unsavory drug habit or perhaps become an international art thief? What was he hiding under that coat? As I hid the lockbox safely in the tent, theories—each more improbable than the last—chased each other around my brain.

Dev was waiting outside, still clutching his jacket tightly together. He looked down the lane, to the left, then to the right. "We walk," he announced.

Silently, swiftly, he led me into the woods, running parallel to the Confederate camp but farther out, in a copse of trees beyond Babbs Mill Road. "Just a little more," he muttered at intervals as we went along. "Just a little farther. Until we're really safe."

"Where are we going to be safe? Florida?" I complained. "Seriously, how far are we going?"

"This'll work." Dev stopped abruptly, in a very dark cluster of woods. "Don't ask me where I got this"—he shook his head—"but look." He opened up his jacket to reveal a Reese's Peanut Butter Cup hidden in his inside pocket.

"What!" I gasped. "How did you—? Where did you—?"

"I said don't ask!" he insisted. "I don't wanna tell you what I had to do to get this." He shuddered. "But one of these is yours, if you want it."

"Oh, Dev, that's so nice of you, but I don't know, eating modern candy—I feel sort of bad. There's only hard-core reenactors here this week; we haven't eaten anything that wasn't roasted on the fire pit—"

"Come on, goody two-shoes." He pulled the Reese's out of his pocket, waggling it temptingly in my face. I had to admit, it did look a whole lot better than the salt pork and flavorless biscuits we'd been subsisting on. I was starting to count down the days until I could get to a gas station and buy some Twizzlers. "It seems like eons since we've had chocolate. We've seen hide nor hair of it. Think of the smell. The melting sweetness. The chocolaty, peanut-buttery goodness." He pressed the wrapper under my nose. Mostly it just smelled like plastic. "Come on, just give it a try. I know you want it. Just one little peanut butter cup." He pulled the Reese's back toward himself. "One little cup won't kill you."

"I don't know. It feels wrong. It's kind of creepy out here," I said, shivering.

"Oh, come on." His forefingers were poised to tear into the package, resting delicately on the crinkly edge. "Stop being such a baby. What're you afraid of, a—"

"GHOST!" I shrieked.

"GHOST!" Dev shrieked in an even higher octave than I did. "Holy shit, ghost!"

"Oh my God," I whispered. Not so far off in the woods, making her way toward the Confederate camp, there was a woman in a long white dress, with dark hair falling in her face. Upon hearing our shrieks, she stopped and turned to face us. It was the single most frightening thing I'd ever seen. I didn't actually pee myself, but for the first time, I understood how someone could be so scared that they would.

"Oh my God, oh my God, oh my God," Dev whimpered. "She came out of the TV like in *The Ring* and into our battlefield!"

"There's no TV here!" I was starting to get hysterical.

"Whatever, she's the one from *The Grudge*—who cares!"

"What do we do, what do we do, what do we do!" Okay, I was definitely hysterical. "We're so far out from the camp!" It was nearly pitch-black, there were trees everywhere, and there was nothing between us and safety but the undead.

"In Georgia, no one can hear you scream!" Dev moaned.

"That's space!"

"Whatever, it might as well be space—there's no one here!"

The ghost took a step toward us.

"Oh my God." I grabbed Dev's arm. "Dev, what do we do? We have to get back to camp."

"You think I don't know that?" He grabbed my arm. We were both clutching each other so tightly, we'd probably cut off our circulation. I sure couldn't feel my arm anymore. "But she's kind of in our path."

"We can't run deeper into the woods," I said firmly. "We'll only get more lost. That was the mistake they made in *The Blair Witch Project.*"

"OMG, don't even THINK *The Blair Witch Project*—this can*not* go down like that." His nails dug into my forearm.

"Think we can outrun her?" I asked. "If we just made a beeline for camp?"

"It's a ghost—can't they, like, go anywhere? Like really fast and through walls and shit?"

"I don't know. I can't think of anything else!" I said desperately.

She took another step.

"Oh my God, do you think she's hungry?" Dev said. "Like, will she drink our blood?"

"It's a ghost, not a vampire!"

"How can you tell?! It's a pale and creepy creature in the woods!"

"I think we have to make a run for it." I set my jaw determinedly. "Maybe a distraction, first? Or something. And then we'll go on the count of three."

"Okay, okay," he said nervously. "Let's do it."

She took another step.

"Screw it, we're going now!" Dev screamed. "Throw the Reese's, throw the Reese's!"

"You have it!" I reminded him.

"Right! Don't eat me! Eat this!" Dev grabbed my arm and pulled me back toward the camp, chucking the Reese's Peanut Butter Cups at the ghost's face as we sprinted past her. We ran as if our lives depended on it, hurtling through the woods at a speed that would have qualified us for the track team. In a fraction of the time it had taken us to get out there, we collapsed, panting, in the glow of the Confederate campfires. I looked back, wheezing in my corset. The ghost hadn't followed us.

At this point, it was after All-Quiet, so there was nothing we could do until the morning. Dev left Captain Cauldwell a strongly worded letter, which led us, after a night of little to no sleep, straight back to a meeting early the next morning at the schoolhouse. Once again, Captain Cauldwell asked the perpetrator to "'fess up," but no one came forward.

"I want an armed guard!" Dev demanded after ten minutes of indeterminate mumblings and ramblings from the men. "Do any of these guns actually shoot?"

"No, that would be a huge safety hazard," Captain Cauldwell said.

"I don't think you can shoot a ghost. It would go right through them," one of the Boy Scouts offered helpfully.

"There's no ghost. There's no such thing. It wasn't a real ghost," Captain Cauldwell said calmly.

"Was too!" Dev shot back somewhat hysterically.

"Are y'all *sure* you didn't just see a lost reenactor and spook yourselves in the dark?" Captain Cauldwell asked skeptically.

"I wish I could say that," I answered, sighing heavily. "And I know this whole story sounds ridiculous, but I really don't think so. It didn't look like a person. It looked like a ghost. And it looked exactly like Jackson described it."

The men muttered. I mean, I knew Captain Cauldwell was right, and ghosts weren't real. Except that this thing . . . whatever it was . . . had certainly looked real. And it looked really, really creepy.

Dev raised his hand. "I still want a bodyguard!"

"If I can be Libby's bodyguard, I'll watch him, too," Cody offered.

"I neither want nor need a bodyguard," I said testily.

"Of course you don't," Dev sniffed. "Clearly, this ghost only has it in for handsome young men. Which is why Corporal Anderson and I have been so egregiously targeted."

"Then I guess she'll be after me next." Cody nodded, resigning himself to his fate. "My days are numbered."

"When I said young, I didn't mean 'still watching *The Wiggles*' young," Dev said snarkily.

"I don't watch the damn *Wiggles*!" Cody yelled.

"Riiiiight," Dev replied sarcastically.

"Order!" Captain Cauldwell banged his fist on the lectern.

"I don't!" Cody muttered mulishly.

"Suuuure you don't," Dev said under his breath.

"I said order!" The room got quiet. "Listen, I can't do anythin' about this right now; we've got a cavalry battle to get to."

"But my *life* is in danger—"

"We're all in danger. Kilpatrick's Raid, son. Can't do anythin' about anythin' else now." Captain Cauldwell held up his hand for silence. "We'll deal with this later. Men, fall out."

Obediently, the men filed out of the schoolhouse, Beau shaking his head as he passed. Dev folded his arms, frowned, and grumpily slouched in his seat, refusing to move. We were alone in the schoolhouse.

"Well, that did nothing," he complained.

"Well, what do you expect him to do?" I said helplessly. "I mean, I don't know what he *can* do. How would you get rid of it?"

"I want it to go away. I expect him to make it go away. And I wasn't kidding about that armed guard."

"Excuse me." A mother with a fanny pack, holding a small child and trailing two others behind her, stood in the door. "Is this the 'Drop the Hanky' Children's Circle?"

"Um, does this *look* like the 'Drop the Hanky' Children's Circle?" Dev snapped.

"Dev!" I admonished him. "Here, let me help you." I picked up a schedule that someone had left on the floor from yesterday. "Yes, you're right—it's in this room, right after Kilpatrick's Raid. Same time as the Ladies' Tea in the Activity Barn."

"Ladies' Tea?" Dev perked up. "You think they'll have coffee?"

"Only one way to find out."

We spent the next hour watching Kilpatrick's Raid, which was marginally more interesting than a normal battle, as it involved more horses. Dev, near delusional from lack of sleep, started yelling, "Save a horse, ride a cowboy!" until the woman standing behind us bopped him on the head with her parasol.

Not surprisingly, Dev and I were first in line for the Ladies' Tea. He marched straight up to the plaid-clad, pagoda-sleeved matronly woman standing at the door of the Activity Barn.

"Pardon me, ma'am." Dev smiled winningly. "You wouldn't happen to have coffee in there, would you?"

"It's a *tea,*" she said icily. "For *ladies.*"

"Humph."

I shrugged. Dev gave up and went back to Sutlers' Row. I joined the ladies for an hour of tea, almond sponge cake, knitting patterns, poetry readings, and a lengthy debate on the attractiveness of a beard. Dev may have gotten the better end of the bargain.

The next day was pretty much like the day before, only the Union corps broke through Hardee's thinning line and crushed the rest of the Confederate soldiers. Eventually, it was all over, and all of the corpses, Beau included, picked themselves up. As they were re-forming their ranks to head back to camp, Beau waved, broke line, and jogged over to meet us.

"How's it going?" Beau asked.

"Tired. Traumatized." Dev sighed. "But really, what's to be expected in my situation?"

"We've gotta do somethin' about this," Beau said, his jaw set.

"About what?" I asked.

"This ghost thing. It's gone too far. We've gotta figure out who's doin' it and stop 'em."

"Thank you!" Dev said. "Finally, someone is concerned for my safety and taking action!"

"Exactly," Beau agreed. "We're gonna take action. And we've gotta catch it. Er, her. It. Whatever."

"Wait, 'we'?" Dev stopped abruptly. "What is this 'we'? I didn't mean 'we' at all. I meant you."

"You ready?" Beau turned to me.

"For what?" I asked nervously. I mean, sure I wanted this whole ghost thing to go away. But I wasn't really sure I wanted to be running around in the woods trying to catch it.

"For the Military Ball tonight," he said with a grin, changing the subject. "Time to break out those dance moves we've been workin' on all week! We'll get down to the bottom of this ghost thing after the party."

"Oh, I don't know," I said anxiously. "I'm so not ready; my waltzing is atrocious."

"It's not atrocious," he said kindly. "It's just not good."

"Thanks."

"Uh, no, wait." He blushed. "I didn't mean—"

"Are you familiar with the phrase 'honest to a fault'?" I teased him. "That was the fault."

"Anderson!" someone yelled. "Let's go, let's go!"

"Sorry!" Beau yelled, as he jogged away. "I really didn't mean it like that!"

"Sure you didn't!" I yelled back.

"I'm not catching anything," Dev said flatly as we walked back to our tent. "The two of you can take your Daphne-and-Fred-style sexual tension and solve whatever you want, but leave me out of this freaky *Scooby-Doo* nightmare."

"There's no sexual tension! Argh!" I smacked my forehead. "How many times do I have to say it? There's *nothing* there! It's all in your head!"

"Hmmm." He fixed me with a look. "So you wouldn't mind

if I just put you in a sack dress for the ball tonight? I don't really want to have to press any of the nicer gowns."

"What, no!" I protested. "I have to look good. I—Wait a minute." Dev was smiling with satisfaction. "Um, no, this has nothing to do with that. I want to look good because it's a dance, and that's what you do. You look nice. And I want to wear a pretty dress. It has nothing to do with anyone else. It's all about me." Dev choked on a laugh. "Wait, no, that's not what I meant either."

"Ah, Libby." Dev slung an arm around my shoulder and kissed my cheek. "I'm finally starting to rub off on you."

Of course Dev didn't put me in a sack dress. It was a stunning off-the-shoulder gown of warm cream, with a cherry-red belt, cherry-red bows on the sleeves, and little blue-and-red cloth swallows pinning back the voluminous folds of the overskirt to reveal an underskirt dotted with a pattern of tiny printed swallows. I pulled on my white gloves as Dev tied a red sash on his Zouave uniform. The Zouaves were French infantrymen in North Africa who favored cropped open-fronted jackets, baggy trousers similar to harem pants, sashes, and bold colors. Units on both sides of the Civil War adopted their names and style of dress. And since this was a Military Ball—meaning anyone with a dress uniform would be in one—Dev felt that included him, too.

"Who doesn't love a crop top?" Dev posed and extended his arm. "Let's do this."

On our way over to the Activity Barn, I felt an unfamiliar vibrating in my corset. My cell phone! It had been so long since I had used it, I had forgotten it was in there.

"Go!" I shoved Dev in toward the ball. "I'll be there in a minute. Just go!"

"Um, okay." He looked sort of confused but went into the Activity Barn without me.

Quickly, I darted behind a tree. I felt around the swallows parading on the front of my bodice and pulled out my phone.

"Garrett!" I whispered. "How are you?"

"Good, good, how are you?" He sounded happier than I'd heard him the last time we spoke. Certainly the happiest he'd been all summer.

"Oh, I'm fine. You sound good. I'm glad."

"I can hardly hear you."

"Sorry," I whispered, slightly louder. "I'm not really supposed to be on a phone . . ."

"Have you seen the *Tuscaloosa News*?!" he asked excitedly.

"What?" Talk about the last thing I expected him to ask. "Um, yeah, I have. Why?"

"Libby! You out here?" It was Beau, calling for me. Shoot. I could not let him catch me with a cell phone. I would lose all my hard-core reenactor cred.

"Garrett, I'm so sorry—I have to go," I said hurriedly.

"But, wait, Libby, I'm trying to tell you. I'm—"

"Sorry!" Guiltily, I snapped the phone shut and shoved it down the front of my dress.

"There you are!" Beau stood before me, straight-backed and tall, resplendent in his uniform. "May I have this dance?"

He held out his hand. I placed my gloved hand in his and followed him in.

chapter five

"Now, where the hell are we?" Dev blinked into the sun. "Ugh, could somebody please hurry up and invent sunglasses? This is killing me. I'm, like, going blind."

"If you're waitin' on the invention of sunglasses, you've got a ways to go. Sam Foster didn't invent them until 1929," Beau commented, as he hammered a post into the ground. "Course, the Chinese darkened eyeglasses by tinting them with smoke back in the 1400s. But they didn't make 'em to protect your eyes from the sun, or reduce solar glare, or correct vision, or anythin'. Judges wore 'em to conceal their eyes while in session in court, so the jury wouldn't have any idea what they were thinkin'."

"Jesus." Dev rolled his eyes. "You're worse than Libby."

I glared at Dev. I mean, come on, that was impressive.

"Sunglasses as we know 'em, glasses made specifically to shield your eyes, are strictly a twentieth-century phenomenon. So like I said, you'd have a ways to wait. And a ways to go. Sam Foster started sellin' 'em up in Atlantic City. Not down here."

"Which is where, again?" Dev asked. "Where is here?"

"Simpsonville, South Carolina." Beau shook the pole, to make sure it was sturdy, before adding, meditatively, "The Golden Strip."

"This is the Golden Strip?" Dev snorted. We stood at the

edge of a dirt road and looked down a long green expanse of not much. "Um, why?"

"Low unemployment, or somethin'." Beau stood up, wiping the dirt off on his pants. "And that's a well-constructed tent right there."

"With a name like the Golden Strip, you'd think there'd be more boutiques and less . . . dirt." Dev rubbed his spotless boots with a silk handkerchief until they shone. "Or at least some strippers."

No boutiques. And certainly no strippers. We were in a field behind the Upcountry South Carolina Historical Society, camping out until the Raid on Hopkins' Farm that weekend. It was a much smaller reenactment, in a much smaller field, with even less to do. Another quiet week under the southern sun.

Dev never got that armed guard. The only people who had volunteered to sleep outside our tent and protect us from the ghost were Beau (whom Dev vetoed, as he was the ghost's primary target and would therefore do more harm than good by attracting the ghost) and Cody (whom I vetoed, for obvious reasons). Even though another Boy Scout had left in the wake of our ghostly sighting, it ended up being for nothing. We hadn't seen so much as a haunted footprint. Nothing even remotely spooky. Not a trace of the ghost.

So there was nothing to do but practice dancing. And I needed all the help I could get. Even by the close of the Friday Night Period Dance, a casual affair in the lantern-lit field, I still wasn't really getting it.

"And one-two-three, one-two-three!" Beau shouted gaily, as we waltzed down the lane. Even though the dance was over, we hadn't been ready to stop dancing. It was one of those perfect summer nights, where everything was bathed in moonlight, and you never wanted the sun to come up. "I said one-two-three! Three, Libby, three! What the hell are your feet doin' down there?"

"I'm trying!" I shouted back. "I told you rhythm is not one of my strong suits."

"See, Beau, you should have danced with me!" Dev shouted from behind us, as he ambled slowly out of the party, to make sure he hadn't missed any hot prospects. There weren't any in Simpsonville.

"Let's do a spin!" I suggested.

"Aw, you ain't ready." Beau grinned.

"Twirl me!" I commanded. "Twirl! Twirl! Twirl!"

He did, and I twirled merrily down the lane, careening directly into the last person I expected to see south of the Mason-Dixon Line.

"Garrett?!" I gasped. "What—Wait—What—How?"

"Hey, Libby," Garrett said warily, eyes on Beau, who had crossed his arms and was looking Garrett up and down, sizing him up. Garrett was taller, but Beau's build reflected a lifetime of football, and Garrett's reflected the approximately eighteen hours a day he spent in front a computer screen.

"What are you doing here?" I regained my composure, getting over my initial surprise, and hugged him tightly. "Oh, it's so good to see you," I said, melting into his arms.

Garrett looked down at me, and his somewhat stony face softened. "You too." He smiled, then cupped my face in his hands and pulled it up toward his. "God, I missed you. You have no idea."

"Me too." He kissed me, and I clung to him, never wanting to let him go.

"Ahem." Someone coughed discreetly in the lane. Oh, right. I broke away, somewhat embarrassed. Beau was scuffing his boot, watching it make little eddies in the dirt. Dev was now practically sprinting up the lane, a manic gleam in his eye, clearly beside himself with excitement at the potential for drama rapidly developing in a random field in the South Carolina upcountry.

"Hey, man," Garrett said gruffly, his already low voice dropping two octaves until it reached a Tom Waits–ian rumble, and slung an arm around my shoulder. "'Sup?"

I shot him a look, as if to say, *Who are you, and what have you done with my boyfriend?* Because I don't think Garrett had ever said "'sup" in his life.

"Ah, yes," Beau said, nodding. "This must be the reporter."

Except with his accent, of course, it sounded more like "re-poht-ah."

Which prompted Garrett to say, "Yep, the reporter." And hit each *r* so hard, they cut through the air like a knife. Couldn't cut the tension, though. Because Garrett then murmured, so low that only I could hear it, "And this must be the reason you hung up on me."

The color drained from my face. "*No,* Garrett," I assured him. "Well, maybe, technically. But not the way you think! Let me explain. It's just that we're not supposed to have cell phones here, and he was about to catch me, so I—"

"So, what brings you to town?" Dev asked cheerily. "Vacationing on the Golden Strip?"

"On the what?" Garrett blinked behind his glasses, confused.

"Welcome to the Glamorous Golden Strip!" Dev flung his arms open wide. "Upcountry South Carolina! The Vacationland!"

"Maine's the Vacationland," Garrett said. "I'm not on vacation. I'm here to see Libby."

I'm not on vacation? I mean, that didn't sound good.

"Wait, is this business or pleasure?" Dev asked for clarification

"Business."

"Not pleasure?" I asked, panicky.

"Burn," Dev whispered.

"No, no." Garrett pushed up his glasses to rub in between his eyes. "The real reason I'm here is to be with Libby. The practical reason I'm here is for work."

"But you work in Boston," I said. This was making no sense.

"That is what I was trying to tell you on the phone," Garrett said, "when you . . . hung up on me." He narrowed his eyes ever so slightly at Beau. "About the *Tuscaloosa News*. It's owned by the *Boston Globe*'s parent company. For weeks now, I've been combing every southern paper that the *Boston Globe* people own, trying to find something, anything, that could get me sent down south, on assignment or on a transfer. And when the *Tuscaloosa News* published that thing about the ghost of Anne Mitchell and the Fifteenth Alabama, I pitched it to my boss. And because I'd gotten the job because of the ghost thing last summer, they agreed to let me cover this."

"You came all the way down here to see me?" I asked in a little voice, my heart melting. I mean, really, talk about romantic! "You transferred from the *Boston Globe* to the *Tuscaloosa News?* For me?"

"Technically, I transferred to the *Tuscaloosa News* in Alabama, the *Spartanburg Herald-Journal* in South Carolina, and the *Lexington Dispatch* in North Carolina. I now have a ghost-hunting, Civil War Unsolved Mysteries–type of column in every southern affiliate of the *Boston Globe*'s parent company. But, yes," he said, and smiled, "for you." I smiled back. "And, well, now I don't have to sit on the floor," he added wryly.

I looked up at him, this sweet, wonderful, amazing boy I was lucky to call mine, and said, "Oh my God, what are you wearing?!"

"What?!" He took a step back, like I'd splashed water on him. "Libby, what!? Are you serious?! I mean, I know you're not crazy about my clothes, but this hardly seems like the time! I haven't seen you in forever, and I thought we were having, I don't know, a moment, or something."

"No, no, not that. Actually, that Ironman shirt's not so bad. It's one of your better ones. Is it new?" It really was nicer than his usual T-shirts, kind of cute, vintage print, and . . . argh! Focus! "No. That's not what I mean. I mean the camp is closed to the public, and you can't be here wearing modern clothes. You'll get in trouble. You have to get out of here!"

"Get out of here? Are you joking?" He looked at me with utter disbelief. "I just drove sixteen hours to see you!"

"No, no, I want you here—you just can't wear *that* and stay here! I mean, where were you planning to stay?"

"Uh, here, I guess." He shrugged. "I need to get to the bottom of this ghost thing, so I'll have to set up a stakeout."

"I think we've got a fine handle on catchin' the ghost ourselves," Beau said evenly.

"Yep, you guys have been doing a great job," Garrett said

sarcastically. "Which accounts for that second article about the ghost terrorizing two civilians, so-called 'close, personal friends of Anderson,' in the woods."

"There was a second article?" I asked. "How? Who's telling the papers?"

"OMG, we were in the newspaper?" Dev asked excitedly. "Was there a photo? Or a sketch of us? An artist's rendering? Anything?"

"No, Dev." Garrett sighed.

"Was my name at least in print?" Dev pouted.

"No, Dev." Garrett sighed again. "But it doesn't matter. Now you'll have official press coverage. And it's not really 'ketching' the ghost that matters." He looked levelly at Beau as he spoke. "I'm here to figure out *why* whoever is behind this is doing what they're doing. To figure out what's happening. Not to just catch it. It's a lot more complex than that. It's not like you can just tackle it."

"Well, actually, I *can* tackle it," Beau said, implying that Garrett couldn't.

"Okay," I said, before Garrett could reply. "This is a problem with an easy solution. All you really need is period clothes. I guess you'll just have to join the unit, or something."

"I'm not joining this unit," Garrett said flatly. "Not in a million years."

"What, you got a problem with Alabama?" Beau stepped forward menacingly.

"No, I've got a problem with people glorifying the most obviously evil violation of human rights in the history of this messed-up country—"

"What, you got a problem with America, now?" Beau interrupted. Oh, dear, this was not going well.

"Hey, clown, what're you doin' with your arm around my woman?" Just when I thought it couldn't get any worse, Cody charged menacingly up the lane.

"Who are you?" Garrett looked down at Cody, who seemed about as tall as his bellybutton.

"I'm Libby's boyfriend." Cody puffed up his chest. "Who're you?" Cody looked him up and down.

"Um, I'm Libby's boyfriend." Garrett shot me the most quizzical look in the history of quizzical looks. One eyebrow had traveled all the way up to his messy hairline, and the other had furrowed so deeply, it was below the plastic rim of his glasses.

"You have got to be kiddin' me." Cody snorted. "Him? Really? This is some kinda weird Yankee joke."

"*You've* got to be kidding!" Garrett said. "Libby, if I knew you were doing God knows what with half the army, maybe I wouldn't have come down here at all! I'm almost expecting them to burst out into 'If You Knew Libby Like I Knew Libby' in three-part harmony or something!"

"Stop it! Just stop! You're not my boyfriend!" I shouted. Garrett's brow furrowed further. "No, no, not you." I patted his chest reassuringly. "You are my boyfriend. *He's* not my boyfriend!" I pointed at Cody. "I'm not a cradle robber! I don't have a creepy *The Suite Life of Zack and Cody* fetish!"

"This is the best summer *ever,*" Dev cackled joyously.

"And Beau and I are *just friends.*" I stood up on my tiptoes so I was slightly closer to looking Garrett directly in the eyes.

"Just friends. There's nothing going on with him or with the midget. The only person I'm involved with is you. The only person I have feelings for is you. The only person I want to be with is you. Okay?"

"Okay," he muttered. It didn't sound particularly convincing, however.

"Garrett, you trust me, don't you?" I asked, sort of hurt and surprised by how doubtful he sounded.

"Yeah, yeah, I trust you." His arm was still around me, and he kissed the top of my head, but it still really didn't feel right. Why was he being so weird and suspicious?

"Well, I'm really glad you're here." I squeezed his hand. "Really, really glad. And I don't want you to leave. So where are you gonna stay?"

"Um, I dunno." He looked from Dev, to Beau, to Cody. "If I stay here, do I really have to wear a costume?"

"'S not a costume," Beau muttered. "It's a uniform."

"Ah, yes, the pretend uniform of the imaginary army for the make-believe war," Garrett said quietly. "Could a band of fairies weave one for me out of unicorn hair?"

"Be nice," I hissed. "But, yes, if you want to stay on the battlefield, you have to wear period dress."

"If I have to." He sighed heavily. "Which way to the *Union* troops?" he asked pointedly, emphasizing "Union."

"Um, that way." I pointed across the field. It was small enough that you could see them easily. "Are you just going to waltz over there and ask a unit of total strangers to take you in? Dressed like that?"

"I've got a press pass. I'll be fine. One of these units will be more than willing to cooperate for the press and let me stay with them and toss me something to wear, in exchange for a positive mention in the paper. Some people just love seeing their name in print."

"How dreadfully shallow," Dev murmured, batting his eyelashes.

"There'll be a unit from Maine. I saw *Gettysburg.* There was that guy who went to Bowdoin, right? We studied him in school, as one of Maine's heroes. They'll be more than willing to, uh, take in a son of the native soil, I bet," Garrett said, and hitched up the messenger bag that was flopping behind him. "I'll see you tomorrow, then, Libby."

He walked off into the night, just as the bugle sounded for All-Quiet. Dev grabbed my hand, and I squeezed his tightly. Wordlessly, we walked off into the dark, toward Sutlers' Row, leaving Beau standing alone in the lane.

"So . . . you wanna talk about it?" Dev asked the minute he'd swished our tent flaps closed.

"Not particularly." I gritted my teeth as I contorted my arms around my back to try to undo the buttons. "Help me out of this, will you?"

"Of course. You *sure* you don't wanna talk about this?" he asked skeptically.

"Pretty sure." Once I was in my shift, I flopped onto my cot, staring up at the dark muslin top of the tent. This just felt like an impending disaster. And it should have been perfect! Spending the summer in hoop skirts with my best friend, my boyfriend, and a new friend who was an even bigger history nerd than I was? It should have been great . . . but it felt like everything was about to go wrong.

"If you're sure . . ." Dev flopped onto his own cot.

After a few minutes of silence, I exploded. "I just don't get it!"

"Don't get what?!" Dev propped himself up.

"I've been, like, perfectly faithful, haven't I?"

"Perfectly," Dev grumbled. "Annoyingly so. Boringly so."

"Like a model girlfriend, right?"

"If you were a model girlfriend, you would have been doing coke and screwing pro athletes. Which would have been a *lot* more interesting. So, no. Not a model girlfriend."

"You know what I mean." I reached over to try to smack him, but my arms were a hair too short to reach across the tent from my cot.

"Yes, I know what you mean, and, yes, you've been a very good girl." He sighed heavily.

"Then why was Garrett being so weird?" I asked plaintively.

"Are you kidding?" Dev asked. "Please. It's so obvious. It's like textbook trust issues. This is the kind of 'Dear Cosmo' that writes itself. You said his ex-girlfriend cheated on him, right?"

"Yeah," I said warily. Dev clearly had a better memory for gossip than I did, even when I was more involved in it than he was.

"So he's obviously afraid you're going to do the same thing and cheat on him, too. He has trouble trusting women now. Especially in the company of handsome manly-man, good old Southern soldier-boy history buffs."

"Well, okay, maybe, but that's not fair," I argued. "I would never cheat on Garrett. I'm not his ex-girlfriend. I'm not Hannah Ho-Bag. He has absolutely no reason to be suspicious of Beau."

"I didn't say it was fair; I said that's what it was." I heard a rustling sound that I assumed was Dev shrugging. "Did you really hang up on him because Beau was there?"

"It wasn't like that," I said with a grimace. "I just didn't want any of the reenactors to see me with a cell phone." I rolled over, away from Dev, to face the wall.

"Okay," Dev said quietly. I was already pretending to be asleep.

After a restless night, we woke to the sound of yelling.

"I'm knockin' on your tent!" It sounded like Cody. "I'm carefully and respectfully announcin' my presence, so I suggest you cover yourself, Libby."

"What the what," Dev mumbled, staggering toward the tent flaps in his union suit. "Why do we only get awoken in the most unpleasant of manners? They might as well just start throwing buckets of water in our faces." He pulled open the tent flap. "Yes, tiny gremlin?"

"Sorry to disturb you, Gramps," Cody said. "But you're gonna wanna see this."

Carefully pulling my quilt up to cover any see-through parts, I followed Cody's pointing arm. There was a large cluster of men standing around one spot in the Confederate camp. Sutlers' Row was right in between the Confederate and Union camps, and because the field was so small, we had a pretty good view of both.

"What are they all doing?" I asked. I mean, random clumps of men were de rigueur here, but not that many, and not all in one place.

"Y'all're gonna wanna see for yourselves," Cody advised. "Put on some clothes and scoot."

"Don't tell me to scoot," Dev said imperiously. "I'll come when I'm good and ready." He swished the tent flaps closed. "All right, let's go hurry and see what this is."

Dev helped me into a plaid day dress with a white Peter Pan collar before pulling on his own pants, shirt, suspenders, and plaid neckerchief. He hauled me out of the tent and dragged me into the field until we stood, breathless, on the outskirts of a cluster surrounding one Confederate tent.

Using skills honed by years of elbowing people in the face to get to the front row of Lady Gaga concerts, Dev effortlessly pushed us to the front of the crowd. Beau and Captain Cauldwell were standing there, regarding the tent with dismayed looks on their faces. Painted smack in the middle of the tent, in what looked like more chicken blood, was an upside-down star inside a circle. An inverted pentagram. I shuddered.

"This is your tent, I take it," I said, patting Beau's arm.

He nodded grimly.

"Excuse me, excuse me." From somewhere back in the crowd, Garrett pushed his way toward the front. "Hey," he muttered breathlessly, moving in to stand next to me as Dev wandered over to examine the tent more closely. "Dammit, I can't believe I missed this," he added in an undertone, running his hands through his hair. He'd made the minimum concession possible to period costume, wearing navy wool pants and a button-down plaid shirt. It wouldn't have looked totally bizarre on a modern street corner, but he was technically historically accurate. "Ghost strikes again. I should've been over here."

"An upside-down star? What is this, like, the stupidest ghost ever?" Dev asked, peering at the bloody pentagram. "Doesn't it know what a star looks like? Only one point points up."

"It's an inverted pentagram," Garrett explained. "It's meant to call upon evil spirits and draw them to us."

"Primarily popularized by Aleister Crowley, the Satan-worshiping occultist, in the late nineteenth and early twentieth centuries," Beau chimed in.

"The inverted pentagram had been an invocation of evil long before Crowley," Garrett challenged.

"Wasn't sayin' it wasn't," Beau shot back.

Sheesh. What was this, a nerd-off? If it had been a joust or something, it might have been flattering or romantic, but this was just lame.

"All right, everyone," Captain Cauldwell yelled. "Let's give the boy some space. We've got a raid to get under way. Move it. Let's move it."

Gradually, muttering, the crowd dispersed, until only Beau, Garrett, Dev, and I remained in front of the satanic tent.

"So, do you have any idea who's doing this?" Garrett asked stiffly after a few minutes.

"If I did, I'd've caught him by now, wouldn't I?" Beau replied testily.

"I mean, it could really be anyone," Dev said, jumping in. "No one would ever notice, because you guys go to sleep mad early." I shot Dev a look. "What?! They do! All-Quiet lights out is like ten p.m. at the *latest.* That's just insane."

"He has a point," I agreed.

"Thank you." Dev sighed. "Wanna help me make a 'Later Bedtime' petition?"

"No, not that." I shook my head. "The camp is very quiet at night, and All-Quiet hours are strictly enforced. People take them very seriously. No one leaves their tent. Anyone could be running around and doing this."

"Hmm." Garrett pulled out a pen and used it to scratch his head meditatively. "Anyone here who doesn't like you? Got a problem with you? Issues? A grudge?"

"Not until yesterday when you showed up," Beau muttered. "Naw, the men seem to like me fine," Beau said at a normal volume. "Well, Randall's got some problems with me, maybe, what with the rank issue, but he'd never do anythin' like this. That kid would take a real bullet for this unit."

"Randall?" Garrett extracted a notebook from somewhere and started feverishly scribbling. "Who's that? And rank issues? What's that?"

"Hell, I don't have time for this." Beau gestured toward the field. "I can't stand around and answer these dumb questions that have nothin' to do with anythin'."

"I can explain," I offered quickly.

"Good," Beau said, nodding. "The men are formin' a line for the raid."

"Oh, of course. By all means. Go ahead. I understand. If you don't hurry, the South might . . . lose," Garrett said drily. "Oh, wait . . ."

The two of them glared at each other for a moment before Beau ran off. Dev cackled audibly.

"Can you *please* try to be nice?" I asked quietly, touching Garrett's arm.

"I'm being perfectly nice," he said stubbornly. "It was a joke. I can't help it if no one has a sense of humor down here. Or understands sarcasm. God, it's worse than I thought. I don't know how you've survived."

"It's not so bad." I shrugged. "But it's better now that you're here," I said, taking his hand.

"Vomit." Dev rolled his eyes. "I'll see you guys later." He sashayed up toward the battle.

"So you found a unit?" I asked once Dev had gone.

"Yep." We strolled up the lane toward the battle together, holding hands. "I joined the Twentieth Maine Volunteer Infantry. I remembered them from that *Gettysburg* movie our AP U.S. history teacher showed us after we took the exam. They're pretty cool, actually."

"Yeah?" I smiled. Garrett had never really taken much of an interest in history before. But maybe now that he was actually living it, he'd understand just how cool it really was. Maybe I'd converted him!

"Yeah." We arrived at the top of the hill, where the skirmish had already begun. "See, at Gettysburg, the Twentieth Maine was in charge of holding down this hill called Little Round Top. They were all the way at the end of the line, alone. No one could help them out. And then Little Round Top came under heavy attack from the Fifteenth Alabama."

I shot Garrett a quick look. He was looking stonily down at the battlefield, at Beau's unit, which was, of course, the Fifteenth Alabama. "They—they did, huh?" I asked nervously. I mean, what are the odds?

"Yep." Garrett clenched his jaw. "Outnumbered at Little Round Top, the Twentieth Maine ran out of ammunition after four hours of fighting. But you know what happened when Alabama came to attack?"

"Um . . . no?" I had sort of a feeling we weren't exactly talking about Little Round Top. And if we weren't talking about this in a completely literal sense, I was kind of offended that I was a hill called Little Round Top in this metaphor.

"They charged down the hill and killed all the Alabamans with their bare hands."

I stared.

"Um . . . cool."

"They won the battle," Garrett concluded.

"Um . . . g-good for Maine," I stuttered. While I wanted Garrett to get more interested in history, this was so not what I had in mind.

Below us, the skirmish concluded, and the troops circled back around to line up for the main battle.

"Ouch!" I yelped as something burning hot flicked against my arm.

"Whoops, sorry, darlin'!"

I turned. It was the Mrs. America Southern belle from the Dixie Acres tent! Smoking in the woods.

"Did you just flick your cigarette ash at me?" I asked in disbelief.

"Real sorry, darlin', didn't see you there." She shrugged.

"Understandable. She's awfully short and easy to miss," Garrett joked. "I keep telling her to grow, but she just won't listen." He shook his head sadly.

I made a noise of mock outrage and contemplated tickling him with a vengeance, until I realized the implication of Mrs. Dixie Acres' reappearance in our lives.

"Are you guys just going to random battlefields, trying to drum up business?" I asked her.

She nodded and blew a stream of smoke out one side of her mouth.

"Where's your tent?" I asked sharply.

"On the other side of the bushes, right off the Historical Society property."

"I've got to take care of something," I said to Garrett as I marched past the bushes.

"Wait, I'll come with you." He jogged to join me as Mrs. America Southern belle stamped on her cigarette with a pair of stilettos that resembled nothing from the nineteenth century. "Are you sure your arm's okay?" he asked with concern.

"It's fine," I replied, as I stormed up to the Dixie Acres tent. Same glittery peach writing. Same white shiny material. I pushed my way in, startled again by the blast of AC, as the man with the suit rose to greet us.

"Why looky here!" he said warmly. "I remember you! Bring your boyfriend along? Maybe in a coupla years, you kids can afford a little piece of Dixie Acres for yourselves."

"Unlikely." I folded my arms. "I read your brochure. What you're doing is reprehensible."

"Offerin' affordable luxury to the fine people of this great nation? That's pretty far from reprehensible in my book." He gave Garrett a look as if to say, *Women.*

Garrett mostly looked confused.

"It's reprehensible if you're building it on top of history!" I continued. "Where exactly are you building?"

"A bunch of minor battlefields. You've probably never even heard of them." He chuckled softly.

"Try me." I narrowed my eyes.

"Well, we haven't sorted exactly which—"

"You don't own any land," I said, with more confidence than I felt, but the look in his eyes confirmed my theory. Thank goodness. It wasn't too late to stop this.

"Not yet," he hissed. "We're just taking pre-orders now. Gettin' enough start-up capital to purchase every inch of square footage we need. And believe you me, we are well on our way."

"You will never get enough money. Look at all these reenactors. Some of these reenactments have been happening for decades. There are *people* here already using the land you're trying to buy."

"People who don't matter," he said dismissively. "People who don't *own* any of this land."

"There are hundreds of us here—" I fumed.

"Hundreds of unimportant people," he interrupted me. "Hundreds of people who don't make the laws and don't have the money to do anythin' about changin' 'em."

"There are still a lot of us—"

"Not enough to matter." He chuckled again. "And I'm bettin' there's less and less of you every day. Y'all are a dyin' breed. And if you think I'm gonna let a bunch of freaks stand between me and makin' millions, you are *dead* wrong, missy. So why don't you go home, take off that silly costume, put on somethin' nice, and let your boyfriend occupy your time. Okay? Y'all have a real nice day, now."

Fuming, I pushed my way out of the tent, with Garrett following me.

"I shouldn't have let him get the last word," I muttered. "I should've—should've said, 'This isn't over' or 'You haven't seen the last of me' or—"

"Or 'Now I'm going to tell my boyfriend what's going on'?" Garrett supplied helpfully.

"Ugh, Garrett, that horrible man is trying to build condos on top of Civil War battlefields!" I exclaimed, as we reached our previous perch on the hilltop, Southern belle nowhere to be seen. "And no one seems to care enough to do anything to stop him. And we can't let him do it—we just *can't.*"

"Developing on historic land, huh?" Garrett whistled. "You'd think there'd be some kind of legislation to stop that."

"Apparently not enough," I said unhappily.

"We'll think of something, Libby," he said seriously, turning my face to his so I was looking directly in his eyes. "We can find a way to stop this. Or at least do our damn best to try."

"Are you guys done being gross?" Dev skipped up behind us. "If you're done hand holding and cooing, I'll stay. I need something normal to look at. All the guys here are fug."

"Fug?" Garrett asked.

"Fug. Fugly. Effin' ugly. Hello?" Dev rolled his eyes with disbelief. Garrett looked blank. "How can you not know what 'fugly' is? Honestly, I should tutor you in, like, social studies. Like, how to be a normal human social."

"Hey, I'm the only one who didn't voluntarily come down here to play Redneck Rodeo. For once in my life, I might be the most normal human in a social situation." Garrett brightened at the thought. "Wow, that's a weird feeling."

"We have a normal human social reason to be here!" Dev said stubbornly. "It's called cold, hard cash."

"And not everyone volunteered." I rolled my eyes. "Just ask Cody."

"Who?" Garrett asked.

"Cody. Libby's jailbait boyfriend," Dev answered. "Wait a minute—that might just make you the world's youngest cougar!"

"I am not a cougar!" I snapped. "Cody's that Boy Scout you met last night."

"Wait a minute." Garrett pulled out his pad and flipped through it. "That's not the kid who that . . . guy referred to, is it?" Garrett clearly couldn't bring himself to say Beau's name. I decided not to push it. "With the rank issues?"

"No, that's Randall," I explained. "They're both Boy Scouts. Actually, neither of them likes Beau that much," I mused.

"Wonder why," Garrett muttered. "What's not to love about some brainwashed, backwater, red-state, racist—"

"Piece of white trash?" Dev supplied helpfully.

"I wasn't going to say that," Garrett said mulishly.

"Right. Save it. Say it to his face." Dev rubbed his hands together.

"Would you please stop trying to turn my life into a *Jerry Springer* episode?" I asked. "Seriously. Stop. Or so help me God, I will tell everyone your first piece of Louis Vuitton luggage was a knock-off." The color drained from Dev's face. "Yes, you heard me right. Don't think I wouldn't do it."

"I'll be a very good boy. I promise." Dev clasped his hands like the little angel he wasn't.

"Thank you." I sighed. "Now, the only person I've ever heard be openly hostile to Beau was Randall. He's the Boy Scout brevet corporal, and Beau's the unit's second corporal, and apparently they both think that they outrank each other, and they argued about it once."

"Really." Garrett looked skeptical. "A twenty-something guy got in an argument with a *Boy Scout* about who has a higher rank in a pretend army?"

"Um . . . yes," I answered, blushing slightly, embarrassed for Beau.

"Jesus"—Garrett shook his head—"that's pathetic. Do you think that's enough of a motivation for this Randall guy to go after . . . um . . . after him? With the ghost stuff?"

"Probably," Dev said, shrugging. "These people have, like, no lives. They take this stuff super seriously."

"They have lives," I chided Dev. "And, yes, they do take it seriously. But Beau's right—Randall loves this unit. I don't think he'd ever do anything to displease Captain Cauldwell. And he's definitely not happy about what's going on with the ghost."

"Got it." Garrett scribbled down a few notes in his book. "And the other one? Cody. You said he doesn't like Beau either?"

"Oh, I don't know," I waffled, not wanting to explain further. "I—uh—"

"Libby doesn't want to say because she thinks you don't trust her," Dev interrupted. "Cody doesn't like Beau because Cody likes Libby, and Cody thought Libby liked Beau, and Beau definitely likes Libby."

"Oh, really." Garrett's face darkened.

"Um, help," I squeaked.

"But it doesn't matter"—Dev waggled a finger at Garrett—"because Libby's behavior has been *exemplary.* You hear me? *Exemplary.*"

"Okay, help me less," I muttered to Dev.

"Hello, I'm defending your honor!" he protested. "She can't

help it if half of the Fifteenth Alabama is in love with her. I mean, hello, have you seen the dress?" Dev gestured to me like Vanna White. "It's all my fault, really."

"He doesn't like me." I sighed. "Beau. Really, Garrett, he doesn't. We're just friends."

"You said," Garrett murmured gruffly. He tucked his notebook back in his pocket. I had a sudden flashback to last summer, when I was explaining to one of my campers that Garrett and I were just friends—no matter what any Jonas Brothers' song said. And look how that had turned out. Despite the hundred-degree heat, I shivered and tried to snuggle in closer to Garrett. He stood as still as a statue, so stony he was almost unrecognizable.

"So, what's the plan now?" I asked tentatively.

"First, talk to the Boy Scouts."

"Good luck with that," Dev interrupted. "They're heinous. Faced with children like that, the reason why you breeders insist on reproducing is beyond me."

"And who's in charge . . . Captain . . . Cauldwell, you said?" Garrett continued.

"Yeah."

"I'll talk to him next, then," Garrett added. "Just keep asking around in general. See if I can pick up any more information."

"Sounds like a plan." I nodded.

"And . . . so far, everything's been solely directed at . . . Beau, right?" Garrett spat his name between his teeth, like it had a bad taste.

"Except for the time that the terrible ghostie stalked us in the woods," Dev said, jumping in. "So you'll probably want to do an article on me, too."

"That's what I was afraid of."

"Um, what are you talking about?" Dev exclaimed. "I am stop-the-presses front-page material!"

"No, not that." Garrett shook his head. "If the ghost keeps going after . . . Beau, then it looks like I'll have to sleep out by Beau's tent," he said grimly.

"Now *there's* a sleepover I'd *love* to get an invite to," Dev cackled.

Before I could reprimand him, an enormous explosion boomed out over the battlefield, decimating the Rebels in a cannonade of Union fire.

"You know," Garrett mused, as we watched every soldier in gray fall to the ground, "I might be starting to like this after all."

As I watched my boyfriend survey the carnage, I had a terrible feeling that the battle between Garrett and Beau might end in serious casualties too.

chapter six

"Libby," a whisper of cherry ChapStick-scented coffee breath caressed my face. I'd been having a strange dream in which Garrett was dressed like Han Solo, but seeing as whoever was breathing on me clearly didn't share Garrett's addiction to Wintergreen Ice Breakers, it definitely wasn't him. "Libby." This time whoever it was shook me.

"What . . ." I groggily opened my eyes to see Dev about an eighth of an inch away from my face, close enough that I could count each eyelash. "Sweet Jesus." I recoiled automatically. "Too close."

"Shhh!" he cautioned. "Look!" He pointed out the window.

I leaned over Dev, pausing to dab at a mysterious wet spot on his lapel where I was afraid I'd drooled a little. I had fallen asleep in Beau's truck on the way to the next battlefield. Though I'd hoped Garrett and I could drive to the next battle together and have some time alone to catch up, the Union troops had packed up and left by the time Dev and I woke up this morning. Those Union troops, of course, included Garrett.

I looked out the window. We passed a T.G.I. Friday's, a Red Robin, and a . . .

"Starbucks!" Dev squealed, nearly jabbing me in the eye in his eagerness to point it out. It was nestled in a strip mall on the side of the road, the green mermaid singing her siren song to Dev.

"Where are we?" I asked sleepily.

"Heaven." Dev sighed.

"Durham, North Carolina," Beau grumbled.

"What a town, what a state!" Dev rolled down his window. "Hello, good people!" he called out. "I bless you all!"

A group of kids loitering outside the gas station mini-mart flipped him off.

"Delightful rapscallions!" Dev rolled up the window, chortling. "My good fellow," he addressed Beau, as we rolled to a stop at a red light. "Might we stop in at that dear little Starbucks? I'd be ever so obliged."

"No."

That was terse. And clearly not the answer Dev was expecting, as he blinked rapidly at Beau, like he couldn't believe what he'd heard.

"But—but—but we've stopped for coffee before!"

"That was different."

"You bet your ass it's different!" Dev's voice was getting increasingly high-pitched and panicky. "This is Starbucks. Real coffee. None of that gas station swill or barely passable Yankee mud. I can get something that ends in 'iatto' and is pumped full of artificial syrups and crowned with a tiara of whipped cream!"

"No."

"But we're so close—"

"When I said no the first time, I meant it, so stop askin'," Beau snapped. I was sort of taken aback. It was a tone I'd never heard Beau use before, but he'd been in a discernibly worsening mood ever since Garrett had shown up. "I don't mind you gettin' coffee when I stop for gas because I have to stop. I certainly don't mind stoppin' to shower like we did this morning, but I'm not takin' you out of my way to a goddamned strip mall, just so y'all can stop and piss around with all that modern bullshit."

We sat for a moment in stunned silence.

"So close and yet so far," Dev whispered, and pressed his nose to the glass, staring mournfully at the Starbucks as the light turned green and we shot by it. I reached over and squeezed his hand, wondering why Beau had snapped at Dev like that. It was totally out of character with his generally sweet disposition.

We drove in uneasy silence the rest of the way to the battlefield, hostility and sulkiness radiating like heat off of Beau and Dev, respectively. I stared ahead uncomfortably, wishing I could just go back to sleep but unable to.

The minute we pulled into another in a seemingly endless series of gravel driveways, Dev flung open the door, leaped out, and slammed it, trapping me inside. Beau turned off the truck and did the same thing. I rolled my eyes and pushed open the passenger door, hopping out after Dev. He was squinting under the broad brim of his white hat, fanning himself vigorously with a round, flat, cambric fan with a wooden handle.

"Where are we?" I asked.

"Bennett Place," Beau answered, as he came around to the back of the truck, slinging his Springfield musket and beat-up canvas duffle over his shoulder.

"I haven't heard of this battle." I came around to get my lace parasol out of the truck bed and popped it open, shielding myself from the sun.

"Wasn't a battle." Beau continued heaving boxes, trunks, and bags out of the pickup. "It was a farm. And the site of a Southern surrender."

"Wait a minute." Dev lowered his fan. "Surrender? So after this, the war was over? I didn't think we were done yet. I don't have enough money yet for a bespoke tailor-made couture suit custom-designed for me in the Lanvin atelier!" He returned to fluttering his fan in distress.

"And the South surrendered at Appomattox Court House," I added. "Not at a farm in North Carolina."

"This was *a* surrender. Not *the* surrender. It ain't over." Beau set his jaw. "Lee actually surrendered the Army of Northern Virginia at Appomattox a few days before the Bennett surrender. And here only the troops in the Carolinas, Georgia, and Florida surrendered. The rest kept on fightin', even though the odds were real bad." He looked straight at me. "Southern boys don't give up easily."

Dev raised his eyebrows high up over his fan.

"Funny, actually," Beau said, as he got the last trunk out of the truck bed. "The last battle of the war was actually a Confederate victory. Battle of Palmito Ranch." He readjusted his grip on his Springfield. "No such thing as a lost cause."

"My, my, my," Dev murmured as Beau marched off, leaving us alone in the parking lot. "Looks like the war is far from over. And here I thought the North had won. But I guess nothing's that black-and-white, is it? Or gray and blue, in this case."

"The North *did* win," I said. "The Confederates just happened to win a battle. The North won the war. And it wasn't a war!" I said crossly.

"The Civil War wasn't a war?" Dev asked archly.

"No . . . it was . . . That's not what I . . . Were we even talking about the Civil War?"

"Weren't we?" he replied levelly.

"I don't know . . . I don't know anymore. I'm just so confused." I slumped against the side of the truck.

"Oh, calm down, there's no need to get all Team Edward/ Team Jacob on me," he said, as he smoothed imaginary wrinkles out of his perfectly pressed pants. "Garrett's jealous, and Beau's smitten, but neither of those things is your fault. Anyone who doesn't fall immediately in love with you is a mad fool." He kissed my forehead. "They can't help themselves. So nothing to worry about—there's nothing to be done."

"You're a mad fool," I said, hugging him. "But thanks."

"You givin' out free hugs?" Cody shouted from across the parking lot. "'Cause I'm next in line."

"Hi, Cody." I sighed as the remaining Boy Scouts marched into the parking lot and filed up next to Beau's truck.

"Don't take that familiar tone with a lady, sir," Randall ordered, as he attempted to wrangle Cody back into his perfectly straight line of Scouts. After the satanic sign appeared on Beau's tent, another Scout had left. It was now only Randall, Cody, and one other brave soul. "We're here to carry your belongings, ma'am." Randall saluted before executing a formal bow.

"Y'all can't order me—I'm the Civilian Youth Coordinator. Emphasis on 'Civilian,'" Cody replied churlishly, as the Boy Scouts gathered up our trunks and hatboxes.

Randall rolled his eyes. "Well, fall out, men. And civilian."

"Excuse me, I'm coordinating these civilian youths," Cody replied, and pulled me away from the truck. Randall picked up our largest trunk and, huffing and puffing, led the other Scout away. Cody lagged behind, still holding my arm like he was escorting me into a dinner party or something.

"You there! Youths!" Dev called after them. "Make sure you pick a prime location!"

"We will, sir!" answered a tiny boy under a stack of hat-boxes. They marched down and disappeared behind the farm-house, an old weather-beaten wooden building at the center of a green pasture ringed by a split-rail wooden fence. All around the house white tents sprung up like dandelions.

"How do you reenact a surrender?" Dev fanned himself idly. "Is this gonna be even more boring than usual? Do we have to watch people sign papers?"

"That's part of it." Cody shrugged. "Mos'ly it's a demonstration of soldier stuff. Discussin' and exhibitin' uniforms and kits and gear and guns and stuff. We just camp out here, and people come an' look at it. Sorta boring. Which is prob'ly why they got Corporal Boring to lead the gun demo this year. He'll be real busy boring people to death all next weekend on the subject of revolvers and rifles—which gives you more time to spend with me." He grinned.

"Corporal Bor—Anderson," I corrected myself, "has no bearing on the time I spend with you. Which remains now, as always, as little as possible." I disentangled my arm. "Shall we, Dev?"

Dev shooed Cody away with his fan and hurried to follow me around to the back of the farmhouse. "I like you all frosty and sassy!" He giggled as we took seats on a bench behind the house. "I knew this Southern belle thing would be good for you."

I batted my lashes and twirled my parasol. He laughed.

"I wonder where Garrett is," I mused. "I mean, it was weird that he didn't want to ride with me, right? That he didn't even ask or try to find me before he left?"

"Libby, stop worrying." Dev patted my knee jovially. "Everything will work out fine."

"You're in a surprisingly good mood, given your Starbucks disappointment," I remarked. "I was expecting an epic sulk. This is uncharacteristically mature."

"Please," he cackled. "Weren't you listening to Beau? There's no such thing as a lost cause."

"Yes, there is. We're kind of living it. The lost cause refers to a postwar mythologizing of the Confederacy as the last bastion of nobility and chivalry."

"Never you fear, Miss Kelting. Starbucks will rise again!" he vowed. "As God is my witness . . ." He raised his fists to the sky. "As God is my witness, they're not going to lick me. I'm going to live through this, and when it's all over, I'll never be decaffeinated again. No, nor any of my folk. If I have to lie, steal, cheat, or kill. As God is my witness, I'll never be decaffeinated again!"

"Easy there, Scarlett." I stood to join him. "Let's keep the lying, stealing, cheating, and killing to a minimum."

"Hopefully it won't come to killing," he mused. "But as for the rest . . ." Fire snapped in his eyes. "I have a plan."

"Oh, Dev, no," I moaned. "Coming from you, those are the four scariest words in the English language."

"Wait here," he ordered.

"Dev—"

"Wait!" he called, as he sprinted away, practically skipping down the pasture.

I could hear the men in the field, singing "The Bonnie Blue Flag" as they set up camp. As they chorused on "Hurrah! Hurrah! For Southern rights, hurrah!" I felt a twinge of guilt. It was so easy to forget here what the war had really been about, ensconced in this fantasy world of pretty dresses and charming soldiers. But Garrett was right. We were essentially glorifying the most inhumane institution in our nation's history, and I worried that no one on the Confederate side really stopped to think about it. I mean, you could talk about Southern rights and states' rights till the cows came home, but that wasn't really what was going on here. It was a moral issue. A question not of states' rights, but of human rights. Civil rights. And I was on the wrong side.

Dev returned before I had really started to examine any of my feelings about this. He was holding a plaid bundle and carrying a pair of tall men's brown riding boots in his other hand. He'd also removed his cravat, vest, and jacket, so now he was only wearing a blue collared shirt, unbuttoned to reveal a bit more chest hair than I'd care to see, and a pair of white linen pants. He looked more like a Banana Republic ad than a Civil War reenactor.

"What is all this?" I asked as he set down the boots.

"If we're busting out of here, we need to go incognito," he said, holding out the plaid bundle. "Put this on."

"Busting out—Incognito—What?" I babbled, as I took what turned out to be a shirt.

"I need to get to that Starbucks, Libby. By whatever means

necessary. And we can't show up looking like we escaped from a Mathew Brady photo album. Hence"—he gestured to his outfit—"we'll be incognito. No one will be able to trace us."

"How will we get there?" I asked skeptically.

"Beau's truck." Dev's eyes gleamed.

"How—*how?*"

"No one locks their car down here. He even leaves the keys in it."

"You mean we're going to *steal* it?!" I squeaked.

"Borrow!" he shouted joyously. "It's not like he needs it! He's not going anywhere, anyway. He won't ever even know it was missing."

"Oh, Dev, I don't know." I shook my head. "This seems like a really bad idea . . ."

"Libby. Please." Tears filled his eyes. "You're my best friend. If you love me, you'll do this for me."

"I—I—Oh, all right." I turned around. "Help me get out of this thing."

"Thank you, Libby, thank you!" he cried, as his fingers flew down the tiny row of buttons on the back of my dress. Sure, I knew it was wrong to steal Beau's truck, but if your best friend won't help you get your heart's desire, then who will?

Luckily there was no one around behind the farmhouse, so I was able to strip down and shimmy into the plaid shirt.

"No pants?" I asked. "Why are there no pants?"

"Look how long it is," he answered, gesturing to the hem. "It's a big shirt, and you're short enough that it looks like a dress. It's longer than some of your dresses at home. And, here," he said, as he pulled a long swath of fabric out of the boot and tied it around my waist. "Now it looks like a shirtdress from Urban Outfitters."

"Really?"

"Really." He cocked his head, considering the dress. "Pretty cute, actually. Now put on these boots."

I unlaced my high-heeled boots and pulled on the plain brown ones he handed to me. "Are these men's boots?" I asked quizzically. "They're so small. I'm a seven and a half, and they fit perfectly."

Dev's cheeks flamed. "It—it doesn't mean anything!" he shouted. "That's an urban legend!"

"Wait a minute . . . these are *your* boots?" I asked incredulously. "How did I not know that you had such tiny feet?!"

"Shut up, shut up!" he shrieked. "We're leaving!"

"Okay, okay. Sheesh."

Dev picked up my discarded clothes and hid them in a box containing a small stack of wood.

We sneaked over to the parking lot, but nobody even noticed we were leaving. The parking lot was far enough away from the campsite that no one could see or hear what we were doing. Plus, they were all busy setting up.

I clambered into the driver's seat. Dev had failed his driver's test four times before giving up, so it was up to me. The keys were waiting in the ignition.

"Oh, why couldn't he have been a cynical, suspicious Yankee who locked his truck," I said, bemoaning my fate.

"Just do it," Dev urged me on, like a devil on my shoulder. "Too late to back out now. Just do it."

"I—I—"

"DO IT!"

The engine roared to life. Almost independently of my own volition, the truck backed out of the parking lot and sped down the pavement to freedom.

"This is insane," I muttered, and turned the wheel to the right.

"Insanely awesome. Fine line between genius and madness," Dev said, as he rolled down the window, sticking his nose out the window like a puppy.

"I had really hoped to *not* commit a Class Three Felony this summer." I checked for cops and sirens in the rearview mirror.

"Relax, Thelma, and enjoy the ride." Dev turned on the radio. Carrie Underwood sang out over the airwaves.

"They died, Louise. They died. Thelma and Louise died."

"'I don't even know his last name,'" Dev sang along, completely off-key, pointedly ignoring me.

I rolled my eyes. We headed on down the road, pulling into the strip mall parking lot as Dev warbled out his last "'Oh no, what have I done?'"

"'Oh no, what have I done,'" I agreed, as I pulled neatly up to the curb, parking right in front of a rhododendron bush spreading over the ground beneath the big windows. I turned off the truck, and we hopped out.

Dev was marching up to the front door, a man on a mission, but before he got there, I placed my hand on his arm and froze.

"What?" Dev stopped and looked at me. "Oh my God, what?!"

I couldn't formulate a response. I was too busy staring, horror-struck, at what was going on inside the Starbucks.

Garrett was sitting at a table near the window, across from a pale, pretty brunette girl. And worst of all, he was holding her hand.

"What the what," Dev whispered. "What the *what?!*"

Garrett scooted his chair closer to her and touched her cheek, before bringing his hand down to hers, so now he was cradling her hands in his.

"This isn't happening," I whispered. "This can't be happening."

"Well, maybe it's—Oh my," Dev broke off abruptly, as Garrett leaned forward and took her in his arms.

"Are they hugging or kissing?" I panicked. "Are they hugging or kissing?! I can't tell!"

"I can't tell either—your boyfriend has a freakishly big head!" Dev panicked right back at me. "How did we not notice his head was so big?!"

"He has a normal-size head. He just hasn't gotten a haircut in a while, and it's humid down here!"

"You're defending him? Now? Really? That hair is a crime in itself!"

"RARF!"

Garrett and the girl broke apart.

"What the hell was that?" Dev whisper-screamed, as we dove into the bushes right beneath the Starbucks window. Before my head cleared the rhododendron, though, I got a glimpse of Garrett and the mystery lady turning their heads to the noise to look out the window.

"RARF! RARF!"

"Seriously, what the hell is that?" Dev whispered.

"It sounds like it's coming from the truck," I whispered.

Dev crawled on his belly like he was in the army, pulling

himself along with his elbows as he cleared the bushes, slunk down over the curb, and crossed the asphalt on the side of the truck farthest from Garrett and the girl. Following in his wake, I crouched and scuttled along like a crab, until we were safely behind the truck.

Slowly rising to our feet, we peered into the truck bed. A hundred pounds of dog looked back at us.

"I forgot about that damn dog!" Dev smacked his hand against his forehead.

"Willie's been in there the whole time?" I asked incredulously. "Like even on the drive to Bennett?"

"You know how much that beast sleeps," Dev said derisively. "We could've driven up the Himalayas, and he wouldn't have woken up. Remember when they made him a guard dog?"

"True."

"RARF! RARF!" He barked happily and thumped his tail.

"Shhh, Willie, shhh." I held out my hand, and he slobbered happily over it. "Quiet, quiet, please . . . good boy . . . quiet."

"This is not good," Dev said flatly.

"Not good at all," I agreed. "We stole a truck and kidnapped a dog. I mean, Beau probably wouldn't have noticed that the truck was gone, but if he thinks someone *stole* his dog, he'll flip."

"He should be so lucky to have someone take this behemoth off his hands," Dev muttered.

Willie cocked his head and whined inquiringly at Dev.

"Oh, just ignore the mean man," I said, patting his muzzle reassuringly.

"Shit!" Dev screamed. "They're coming out!"

With a burst of adrenaline known only to mothers whose babies are trapped under cars, Dev and I somehow managed to override our mutual lack of athletic ability and vault over the side of the truck, so we were lying flat in the pickup's bed, hidden by that panel thing in the back and Willie's enormous mass. I wove my fingers through Willie's hair, willing him to keep quiet, as Dev tried to hide himself under the dog. Willie, overjoyed that Dev was finally attempting to snuggle, lay down on top of him, crushing him.

"AAAAA!" Dev gasped. "I can't breathe!"

"Then you shouldn't be talking! Save your oxygen!"

I peeped up over the truck bed. Luckily, both Garrett and the girl had their backs to me.

"Are they hugging or kissing?" Dev had managed to work his way out from under the dog to pop up next to me. "I still can't tell! Curse that bigheaded fool!"

"He—he has a normal-size head," I said again, as they broke apart and got into their respective cars. She, however, was tiny like a fairy. Delicate. She looked a little like Kristen Stewart, from the *Twilight* movies.

"You have two options," Dev said sternly. "Follow him, or follow her."

"Dev, that's crazy." I shook my head. I had a sick, swooping feeling in my stomach, and the world wouldn't stop spinning.

"Of course you're right—that's crazy." He smacked his head. "Follow her. No question. Text him to see what he's doing."

"Dev, I'm not going to—"

"Follow her," he ordered.

"Fine," I said listlessly. I didn't have the energy to fight.

After making sure that Garrett couldn't see us from his car, Dev practically dragged me out of the truck bed and deposited me in the driver's seat.

"It's the silver Kia," he instructed, as I turned the car on. "She's about to turn out of the strip mall parking lot. Go, go, go!"

I went, went, went. My body remembered how to drive, even though my mind was a million miles away. She turned left out of the strip mall, and so did we.

"Give me your cell phone," Dev commanded when we stopped at a red light.

"What?" I asked.

"Oh, sweet Jesus, you are *so* lucky you have me." He leaned over and reached down my bra.

"Hey! Too close!" I shrieked.

"*Now* you're waking up," he said, as he pulled out my cell phone. "Lucky for you, I am an *expert* at cheating assholes. Seeing one, being one, stalking one, blocking one . . . but blocking on Facebook is, like, step five, so don't even think about that yet. This is only the first test. Text him to see where he says he was. Don't worry, I'll do it." He held up the phone. "Hands on the wheel, Thelma."

"Don't text anything dirty, Louise," I warned.

"Please," he scoffed. "That's Phase Three. We're only on Phase One. How's this," he asked, typing rapidly. "'Hey, where r u?'"

"That's fine." I shrugged.

The phone vibrated almost instantly.

"'At Starbucks,'" Dev read.

"See!" I brightened. "See, he's not lying! If he told the truth about that, it probably means there was nothing going on with that girl, right?"

"'Skyping my editor,'" Dev finished. My face fell. "Oh, poodle." Dev turned to me sympathetically. "I'm so sorry."

"He—he didn't—he didn't even have his computer out," I whispered. "So he definitely wasn't Skyping anyone . . . That's not . . . that's not good that he lied, is it?"

"Not good at all." Dev shook his head. "Not good at all."

We turned down a road, passing a blue sign that read DUKE UNIVERSITY SCHOOL OF MEDICINE.

"Med school?" Dev said. "Huh."

The Kia pulled into a parking lot where a temporary sign saying DUKE UNIVERSITY SCHOOL OF MEDICINE SUMMER AND DENTAL PROGRAM had been stuck in the ground. We pulled in and parked behind a large Duke van, hidden from the Kia.

"She's so skinny," I said quietly, as we watched the Kia girl cross the parking lot and walk into the building, her light blue scrub pants and faded gray T-shirt practically hanging off her thin frame.

"You have a better rack," Dev said loyally.

"Thanks," I mumbled.

"Stop." He held me by the shoulders and looked into my eyes. "Don't do this. You are prettier than a pre–Tony Romo Jessica Simpson. Prettier than a pre-rehab Lindsay Lohan."

"Thanks, Louise." I squeezed his arm.

"The adventure's just beginning, Thelma," he said, unbuckling his seat belt. "I'm going in."

"Wait, what?!" I sat up. "What are you doing? You can't go in there!"

"Sure I can," he said confidently. "I'm Indian. Walking into a med school. I was born to go undercover here. Everyone will just assume I'm meant to be there."

"Dev—"

"Give me ten minutes. I'll find out everything we need to know." He leaped out of the car and strode confidently into the building.

My cell phone remained on his seat. I picked it up. There it was: "At Starbucks. Skyping my editor." I rubbed at it with my thumb absent-mindedly, but that wasn't going to erase it. Unable to help myself, I texted, "I miss you."

I clutched the phone desperately, willing for it to vibrate, clinging to it like a lifeline, but no. Nothing.

I have no idea how long I sat staring at that phone, but eventually Dev bounded back in.

"Okay," he said breathlessly. "So I was doing fantastically, totally blending in, then this mouth-breathing moron with a clipboard comes up to me, says he's organizing a softball game, and needs to know who my supervising professor is so he can put me on a team. So I said House. Dr. House."

"Like the TV show?"

"It was the first thing that popped into my head!" he protested. "Then he asked my name, and I said Kal, Kal Penn."

"The Indian actor who played one of the doctors on *House*?" Sometimes Dev was just unbelievable.

"I was thinking off the cuff, okay?!" Dev raised his hands. "Sue me! I did the best I could. Anyway, they kicked me out."

"Oh, Dev—"

"But not before I got . . . this!" He held up an ID on a lanyard. "Ta-da!"

"Dev!" I gasped. "You stole her ID?! How could you?!"

"All's fair in cheating and ho-bags," he exclaimed. "Does the name Hannah Rupp mean anything to you?" he said, glancing at the ID.

"Hannah Rupp . . . Hannah Rupp . . ." I cast around in my brain. "No, I don't think so."

"Hannah Rupp. Pharmacology and Cancer Biology intern." Dev looked up, and his eyes locked with mine. "Camden Harbor, Maine."

"Oh my God," I whispered.

"Wasn't Garrett's high school girlfriend named—"

"Hannah," I finished for him. "Oh my God. Oh my *GOD!* Why is she here?!"

"She's pharmacologizing and cancer biologizing!" Dev said.

"I mean, I mean, why was *he* here?! There! Why would he see her?! She cheated on him! And broke his heart! And . . . and . . . they were hugging!"

"Or kissing," Dev said matter-of-factly.

"Dev!" I wailed.

"Sorry, sorry!" he said.

"Garrett's cheating on me . . . I can't believe it . . . I . . . H-he's cheating on me," I stammered.

"He's the world's biggest idiot," Dev said, squeezing my knee.

"Do you think he's cheating on me because he thinks I'm cheating on him? Is that why? Do you think he thinks I'm cheating on him with Beau?"

"Who can tell what that crazy bastard thinks. I mean, he wears sandals with socks!" Dev shouted.

"That only happened once!" I shrieked. I took a deep breath. "I have to get out of here." I shook my head, trying to clear it. The truck roared to life, and I peeled out of the parking lot so fast we burned rubber.

"Easy there, tiger," Dev cautioned as we sped down the road, trees flying by in a green blur.

"I can't believe he'd do that to me," I muttered. "How could he *do* that to me? I thought he really . . . I mean, I know I really . . ."

"Hey!" Dev said brightly. "Happy place. Let's sing!"

He turned the radio up, and it played: "I'm giving up on love 'cause love's given up on me."

"'I'm giving up on love 'cause love's given up on me,'" I sang. "Perfect."

"Now, this is not exactly what I meant—"

"Don't you DARE change that station!" I shouted, as the woman continued singing.

"I was kind of hoping for something that wasn't about setting things on fire," Dev muttered.

"Nope, this is perfect."

We sped down the road, traveling faster and farther as Miranda Lambert sang about soaking things in kerosene. I knew exactly how she felt.

"Um, Libby," Dev ventured after a while. "Do you have any idea where you're going?"

"Nope," I said evenly. "I just know I can't go back to that camp yet."

"Fair enough." Dev nodded. "Wait! Here! Here! Pull in here! Turn right!"

I did and, tires spinning, we skidded to a stop.

"'The Snikering Squirrel'?"

"I think it's supposed to be 'Snickering,'" Dev said, squinting at the neon sign. "Let's go."

"What is this place?" I asked as we got out of the truck. It was a rambling wooden building that looked like it was about to fall apart at the seams, neon beer signs gracing its windows. "A bar?"

"Nope." Dev pointed at the flashing neon KARAOKE NITE sign. "It's your salvation."

"I'm not in the mood." I scuffed the dirt in the driveway.

"Trust me, I know what's best for you," Dev said, as he dragged me up to the door. "You need to sing this all out. It's the only way for you to deal with your problems. It always helps the kids on *Glee* deal with their issues."

"Dev, we're not twenty-one," I said apprehensively, as we crossed the threshold.

"I don't think that'll be a problem." He glanced pointedly in the direction of a family of four, where two boys who couldn't have been more than eight pelted each other with chicken wing bones.

"My phone!" I cried, feeling a sudden vibration.

"I'll go set this up," Dev said, and disappeared into the crowd.

I pulled it open. It was from Garrett: "Yeah, me too. Where are you?"

My heart thumped. I didn't know what to say. Or if I wanted to see him. But I typed, "At a bar."

I closed the phone and stuck it in my bra. I still didn't really know how I felt. Not that it mattered. Because with only that much information, there was no way he could find me, anyway.

"Libby!" Dev hailed me from the back of the bar. "Come on back!"

I pushed my way through. It was pretty crowded and noisy, with everyone laughing and having a good time. Dev was perched on a barstool at the end of the bar, making goo-goo eyes at a very cute boy in a plaid cowboy shirt.

"That was fast," I muttered.

"Libby, this is Duane," Dev announced proudly. "Duane, Libby; Libby, Duane."

I nursed a soda as Dev and Duane flirted away. Dev managed to get a Sex on the Beach out of Duane with a wink, but I was fine with my Sprite. As I sucked meditatively on my straw, Duane talked on and on about hunting, which Dev kept accidentally-on-purpose mishearing as "humping." A woman got up and sang "Goodbye Earl." A man followed after her and sang "All My Ex's Live in Texas." And then, over the microphone, a man said, "Libby?"

"That's you." Dev slurped up his drink. "Go get 'em, doll."

"Libby?" the man called again.

I made my way to the stage. A somewhat pudgy guy in a cowboy hat handed me a microphone. Slightly tinny opening chords blared out of the karaoke machine. I looked at the screen. Carrie Underwood. Thankfully, it was the only country song I knew. I looked out at the audience, and standing in the door was one of the last people I expected to see. I took a deep breath and sang:

"Right now he's probably slow dancing
With a . . . brunette tramp
And she's probably getting frisky."

Okay, so I know the lyric is "bleached-blond," but somehow "brunette" just popped out.

"Right now, he's probably buying
Her some fruity little drink
'Cause she can't shoot whiskey."

As if I had somehow conjured him out of thin air, Garrett stepped into the bar. How had he found me?

"Right now, he's probably up behind her
With a pool stick
Showing her how to shoot a combo
And he don't know."

By this point the entire bar had stopped what they were doing, and they were watching me, swaying and shouting. The whole room was blurry, except for Garrett. He was the only clear figure in a sea of whirling faces. I tried my best to shut him out and sing.

"I dug my key into the side
Of his pretty little souped-up four-wheel drive
Carved my name into his leather seats
I took a Louisville slugger to both headlights
Slashed a hole in all four tires . . ."

I took a deep breath, looked right at Garrett and sang:

"Maybe next time he'll think before he cheats."

I finished the song, closing my eyes and trying to pour everything I was feeling into the timeless words of Carrie Underwood. The bar erupted into applause, people shouting and stamping and chanting my name. I didn't care about any of that. I couldn't think about anything but Garrett. I handed the mike to the pudgy man and made my way back to the bar.

"Woo-wee!" the man with the mike hollered. "Let's give it up for little Miss Libby!" The bar exploded into cheers again. "Careful not to burn down the bar, girl! You've got some smokin'-hot pipes!"

I nodded and smiled halfheartedly at the guy, while I looked around for my soda. It had disappeared. Dev and Duane were at the end of the bar, making goo-goo eyes at each other.

A female bartender in her forties with frosted hair approached me. "Can I get you somethin'?"

"Whiskey." I mean, that was what one drank in these situations, right? Isn't that what Carrie Underwood had said?

Garrett appeared behind me.

"ID, hon?" the bartender asked, arching a perfectly stenciled eyebrow that framed her crescent of lavender eye shadow.

"Shirley Temple. Straight up. No, on the rocks," I amended.

Garrett slid onto the barstool next to me. "Make it a double."

"Sure thing." She narrowed her lavender eyes at Garrett, as if she recognized when a man had done a girl wrong, and went to fix my drink.

"Hittin' the hooch pretty hard there, huh?" Garrett nodded

at the bartender, who was plopping maraschino cherries into my glass. "Did I just hear you order a whiskey?"

"Maybe."

The bartender slid me my pink glass, and I took a long swig.

"That was quite the . . . um . . ."—Garrett swallowed noisily—"spirited rendition of 'Before He Cheats.' "

"Mmmm." I narrowed my eyes at him. "I really, *really* empathize with Carrie Underwood. So I sang it with feeling."

"That you . . . that you did." He nodded.

"How did you find me?" I asked.

"Google Maps search of every bar in a ten-mile radius. And I have GPS on my phone." He waved it in my face.

"Good for you," I said sarcastically. "Good for you."

"Yeah . . ." He looked at me searchingly. "Libby . . . are you . . . are you okay?"

"Oh, me?" I laughed hollowly. "I'm good. Really good. Good in the sense that I'm doing great, and I'm a good person. *I'm* a *good* person, Garrett."

"I know you are," he said, his brow furrowed. "Libby, what's going on?"

"I need to find Dev." I stood up abruptly. I couldn't talk to him. I couldn't even look at him anymore.

"Uh—okay," he said. "I'll be right here!" he called after my retreating back.

I hopped off my barstool and stalked over to tap Dev on the shoulder.

"You rang?" Dev turned around, after winking at Duane.

"We need to go," I said. "Garrett's here."

"WHAT?!" Dev exploded. "How DARE he?! How dare he come on our turf! I mean, hello, this is practically *our place!*"

"Whatever, let's just go," I mumbled, glancing nervously at Garrett. "I just want to go."

"Oh, we're going all right." He swept off the barstool. "Duane, you feel free to call me."

Dev and I pushed our way out of the bar, Duane waving sadly goodbye.

"Libby!" I heard Garrett call. "Libby! Hey, Libby! Where are you going?"

"Just keep walking." Dev steered me forward. "Just keep walking."

We made it to the truck. I left Garrett standing in the parking lot and sped out onto the road. Aside from the low hum of the radio, Dev and I drove back to camp in silence. Until . . .

"Holy Mary, Mother of God," Dev whispered. "We are in deep, deep shit."

There was a familiar figure in gray leaning against the fence in the parking lot.

"Oh, no," I whispered. "Oh, no, no, no, no, no."

Beau was standing with his arms crossed, and he did not look happy.

"We're sure none of the guns here have real bullets in them, right?" Dev asked.

"Let's hope not."

Dev and I quietly got out of the car, like we were about to head into the principal's office. I let Willie out of the truck bed, and he bounded happily to Beau's feet. I followed slightly less joyously.

"What," Beau said tensely, "the hell were you two *thinking?!!*"

"We were getting—oh my God, I didn't even get my coffee!" Dev cried.

"This was about *coffee?!*" Beau asked incredulously.

"It started off being about coffee," Dev replied.

"Beau," I said, shaking my head, "I am so, so, so—"

Another car pulled into the parking lot. "Libby!" Garrett shouted out the window as he parked.

"Things just got a little out of hand," I said, as Garrett jogged over to join us.

"All right, what the hell is going on?" Beau asked.

"Exactly." Garrett nodded vigorously. "What the hell is going on?!"

"Is that my shirt?" Beau asked out of the blue.

"You're wearing his shirt?" Garrett's jaw fell open.

"Is this his shirt?" I asked Dev, panicking.

"You stole my truck, my dog, *and* my shirt?" Beau asked incredulously.

"We *borrowed* your truck, your dog, and your shirt," Dev clarified.

"Why did you borrow *his* shirt?" I hissed.

"Why did you borrow *his* shirt?" Garrett thundered.

"Because I—Wait a minute!" I whirled around to face Garrett. "*I* don't have anything to feel guilty about!"

"Why are you wearing his shirt?!" Garrett asked again.

"Maybe I have another person's shirt on my chest, but at least I . . . I don't have another *person* on my chest!" I said heatedly.

"Good one." Dev rolled his eyes sarcastically. "Seriously, Libs, not your best."

"What? Who? Chest? What? Who?" Garrett hooted like a confused owl.

"*I* don't have to explain *anything* to *you!*" I shouted. "GOOD NIGHT!"

Garrett took a few steps back, muttered something, and hopped back into his car.

Dev flashed me a thumbs-up. "Maybe slashing-tires time?"

"Maybe later." I shook my head. "Beau"—I turned to him—"you, on the other hand, I have a lot of stuff to explain to you."

"No, she doesn't," Dev interrupted. "It was all my fault. I coerced her. At gunpoint."

"Oh, Dev—"

"Run along, you," he said, kissing me on the cheek. "It's been quite a night. I'll take the heat."

I squeezed his hand, and, leaving all the boys behind, I disappeared into the night.

chapter seven

"What the hell is this?" I tugged unsuccessfully on my bodice, trying to pull it up higher.

"It's an outfit," Dev said, tugging it back down.

"What am I supposed to be? A common whore?"

"Exactly." Dev nodded with satisfaction. "A wayward sister, a soiled dove, a public woman . . ."

"Um, no." I started fiddling around, looking for a way to escape from this scarlet monstrosity. "I'm not going out dressed like a prostitute."

"Sure you are. Stop looking for buttons and hooks—you can't get in or out of that thing without my help." He had a point. It was so tight, he might as well have sewn it onto my body. Which, come to think of it, he actually had done in places.

"Why are you doing this to me?" I asked. "Why, Dev, why?"

"I wanted to let people know you're back on the market!" he exclaimed.

"Back on the market doesn't literally mean 'for sale'!" I protested. "Also, I mean, I'm not technically back on the market. I don't think."

"You have got to be joking." He placed his hands on his hips. "He cheated. C-H-E-A-T-D, cheated."

"You missed an *e*."

"Maybe I'm wrong about spelling, but I'm right about this,"

he said, as he fluffed my hair. "He cheated. He lied. He's a bastard in nerd's clothing. Shut it down, Libby. Shut. It. Down."

"I'm just saying, we haven't officially broken up yet. We should probably talk about this—"

"What's there to talk about?" Dev said, exasperated. "It's over. You don't owe him anything. Not even a conversation. Get out now, before he hurts you any more. And I refuse to let that happen."

"Thanks, Dev."

"Seriously." Dev cupped my chin in his hand. "You deserve someone so much better. A good guy. Who'll treat you the way you should be treated. Who's nicer. Not to mention hotter and better dressed, but those are ancillary issues." He waved his free hand. "I'm not going to let him hurt you again. I'm not going to let you put yourself in a position to get hurt again. Because if he does hurt you again, my vengeance will be terrible. Yea, I swear it. On the hammer of Thor."

"'The hammer of Thor,' huh?" I smirked.

"You betcha. I mean business." He pinched my cheek. "Plus, I thought you'd be into the whole hooker thing! It's super historically accurate!"

"Is it?" I frowned down at the scraps of fabric Dev was trying to pass off as a dress. "Then why do I bear such a strong resemblance to Megan Fox in *Jonah Hex*?"

"No, I meant prostitutes are super accurate, obvi," he said, rolling his eyes. "The Civil War spurred the largest prostitution boom this country has ever known! Wherever the army went, prostitutes were sure to follow!"

"True, but—"

"I mean, if it were *really* eighteen-sixty-whatever and you were following the army, you probs would have been a prostitute," he said with a shrug.

"No way!" I protested.

"A single, unemployed teenage girl following around a bunch of soldiers?" Dev arched an eyebrow. "Riiight . . ."

"Shut up!" I smacked him. "I'm a lady." I looked down at my outfit. "Um, appearance to the contrary . . ."

"Let's show you off," he said, and held open the tent flap.

"I kind of hate you right now. A little bit." I followed him out into the sun.

"Shut up, you love attention almost as much as me—you just won't admit it." Dev patted me fondly. "And you know you look insanely hot. And thusly, we will make that rat bastard curse the day he was born."

"Thusly?" I smiled. "My, oh my."

"It's all part of the plan." Dev pointed to his temple. "Crafty. Use your hotness to torture the man who done you wrong. It's a classic maneuver. One I'm a master of."

"I don't know why I don't fight you more."

"Because you know I always win," he answered smugly.

"Oh, wait," I remembered suddenly. "Do you have the—"

"Yep," Dev answered, shoving a small fabric package at me. I took it. "What are we doing today?"

"Moving on. To the Battle of Bentonville. Four Oaks, North Carolina, I think?" I said, squinting into the sun.

After the whole truck-stealing/boyfriend-cheating debacle, Dev and I had basically been hiding out in our tent as we camped out at Bennett Place. Dev was avoiding Beau, who had been placated but was still annoyed at our grand theft auto, and I was avoiding Garrett, because even thinking about seeing his face made me feel queasy. But another battle day had rolled around, and it was time to leave our sequestered tent. Not like we were going far—Bentonville was less than two hours south—but still. Out into the sun.

A soldier walking by whistled at me.

"That's it, I'm changing." I turned around.

"No, no, Libby, stop!" Dev grabbed my arm. "It takes too long to get you out of that. Think about how historically accurate you are! You know, the term 'hooker' even comes from the Civil War!"

"Actually, that's a common misconception," Beau said, as he strolled up to our tent. "General 'Fighting Joe' Hooker did have a sizable number of female camp followers, ladies of ill-repute, known as 'Hooker's women,' or 'Hookers,' for short. So that would be a nice easy explanation, except the word 'hooker' showed up a bunch of times before the war. In the *Dictionary of Americanisms* of 1859, even back in a New York police report in 1835. It might come from Corlear's Hook, a part of New York that used to be full of brothels, or an even older British slang term for thieves who used hooks to steal things. And, well, prostitutes use more of a metaphorical hook to lure in clients."

"God you're a font of useless information." Dev shook his head.

Beau folded his arms and glared.

"I, mean, uh, fascinating," Dev said, clearing his throat. "And on that note, I'm getting 'coffee,'" he said, using air quotes.

Dev scuttled away hastily. Beau and I shuffled awkwardly in

front of each other; he looped his thumbs through his suspenders as I tugged nervously at my bodice.

"Boys'll be along any minute to take down the tent," he said, and nodded.

"Thank you, I, um—I have an 'I'm sorry' gift. For you," I blurted out.

"Is it the outfit?" A grin spread slowly across his face. "Because if it is, apology accepted."

"Oh, God, no," I said, blushing. "Blame Dev for this. He wanted to let people know I was 'back on the market.'" I rolled my eyes.

"Are you?" he asked hesitantly.

"Oh, um, I—I don't know," I stammered. "Um, anyway, here."

I shoved the parcel at him. He unwrapped it slowly, the buff-colored sash falling nearly to the floor.

"It's an officer's sash," I explained. "You know, like Melanie gives Ashley in *Gone with the Wind*? Dev made it. We noticed you didn't have one. And the handkerchief's from me." I pointed to the small white square that was left once he'd unwrapped the sash. "I'm not as good at sewing the big stuff as Dev is, but I'm pretty good with an embroidery needle. I did your initials and your rank and the regiment, see? All in gray."

"I see." Beau smiled, and it crinkled the freckles across his nose. I smiled too. "Thank you, Libby, they're beautiful." He tucked the handkerchief in his pants pocket and draped the sash over his arm.

"You can wear the sash at Bentonville. With your jacket," I suggested.

"That, uh, might prove difficult," he muttered blackly.

"Why?"

"I'll show you later," he said quickly, as if eager to change the subject. "Listen." Beau took a step closer. "Dev told me about what happened with . . . you know, Garrett."

"Oh. Um. Oh." The color drained from my face. Argh, Dev! Why did he say anything?

"Yeah." Beau shook his head. "The only reason I didn't beat the crap outta him is Dev told me you prefer to take care of that kind of thing yourself." A smile began to play across his lips. "I heard some crazy story 'bout you breakin' some guy's nose at a party last summer."

"I didn't break his nose!" I protested. "There was just a little blood."

Beau's eyebrows traveled up to his hairline, and his laugh rang out loud and clear across the field. With that sound, I felt some of the tension in my chest start to loosen.

"Total swill," Dev commented as he returned, clutching a tin mug. "Near undrinkable. Let's hit the bricks so we can meet some Yanks with real coffee."

"I was thinkin' the same thing." Beau cupped his hands around his mouth and yelled across the field. The three Boy Scouts trooped up to dismantle our tent, as everywhere around us tents came down. Dev and I moved to the side, trying not to get in the way.

Cody looked like Christmas had come early. Randall alternated between staring at me slack jawed and looking extremely flustered. Dev chuckled into his coffee, clearly thrilled at the reaction my outfit was getting.

I was done with the ogling. As I marched out of the camp,

Willie followed at my heels. Fine with me. He was the only boy I was really in the mood to spend time with.

Not long after, nothing remained of the camp but an empty field, and Beau and Dev joined me at the truck, ready to head on to Bentonville.

"As punishment," Beau announced, "Willie's sittin' in the front with you. On your lap."

"Fine." Dev nodded. "Libby? You take him."

"No, not Libby, you," Beau said, as he hopped into the truck. "He's all yours."

"This is—this is inhumane," Dev fussed, as we all piled into the car, with Willie snuggling happily on top of him.

"You wanted to be with him bad enough to kidnap him—he's all yours," Beau said smugly, as we pulled onto the road. Dev pouted into a mass of fur.

Something was under me on the seat. I hadn't noticed at first, distracted by all the scarlet silk, but now I could definitely feel something under there. I wriggled around for a bit and pulled it out.

"What is this?" I asked, examining a shredded gray mass of fabric. It looked like fabric papier-mâché.

"Remember when I told you it might be hard for me to wear my jacket?" Beau said. "Well, that's why."

"Wait, this is a jacket?!" I turned it around, trying to make sense of it. I couldn't find any cuffs or collars or anything. It just looked like a random pile of scraps.

"*Was* a jacket," Beau clarified.

"Lemme see! Lemme see!" Dev stretched his arms out around Willie. "I can't see anything but beast fur!"

"What happened to it?" I kept turning it over, looking at

the thick, angry slash marks. "Did an animal get it or something? A raccoon, maybe?"

"Pffff!" Dev spat out a mouthful of fur and clawed his way out so that his head was visible. "That was no animal. Didn't you learn anything from *Twilight*? Vampire!" he proclaimed. "Or in this case . . ."

"Ghost?" I supplied.

Beau swallowed but said nothing.

"You really think this was the ghost?" I continued. "Beau, this looks . . . violent."

"Well, we all know this ghost ain't exactly my biggest fan." He laughed darkly.

"Have you told anyone?" I kept going.

"Naw, not yet—"

"Beau, you have to tell someone!" I interrupted. "Because this looks awful. Scary. I don't want you to get hurt."

"By a ghost?" He laughed. "I ain't too worried. I didn't want to tell anyone, get everybody all worried again. I don't wanna lose any more of the kids. We're down to three! If whatever it is comes after me, I can handle it. A little wardrobe malfunction doesn't scare me. I'll get another jacket. It's no big deal."

"It is a big deal!" I countered. "What if whatever did this to your jacket tries to do this to *you!* Slash you up like that? You have to tell someone!"

"Who? The Ghostbusters?" Dev piped up archly.

"I understand if you don't want to scare the boys, but shouldn't you at least tell Captain Cauldwell? And—and the newspaper?" I stuttered.

"Aw, hell, Libby, is that what this is about?" Beau hit the steering wheel angrily. "You wanna help that asshole with his story? Really? Still? That bastard's gotta be the biggest idiot alive, to screw things up with you! I don't know what the hell's wrong with him!"

"Me neither," Dev agreed emphatically through a mouthful of dog fur.

"It's not about that—it's about . . . um . . . journalistic integrity," I said weakly.

"It's about a load of bull crap is what it's about," Beau muttered.

After that, the ride fell into an awkward silence. It was only about another hour to Bentonville, but it was a bleak hour, into a rural nothing that felt emptier than anything before. We turned off the highway by a gas station boasting PEA AND BUTTER BEAN SHELLING and PINE BALES—DISCOUNT PRICES! next to a sign that read BATTLEFIELD—17 MILES.

It was a long seventeen miles. Nothing but empty fields and modular homes, with a few enterprising businesses sprinkled in between.

"Libby, I think we're actually on the road to *Deliverance* this time," Dev whispered. "'Lee's Hill Welding'? What the hell is 'hill welding'?"

"No, it's . . . it's cute," I whispered. "Just look at the signs for the farm stand."

There were wooden signs spaced all down the road, advertising produce at a farm stand. Bored, Dev read them out as we went past and turned them into a kind of song.

"Hoop cheese. Butter, corn, peas," Dev sang tunelessly. "Cashews, peanuts, pecans, walnuts."

Willie whined.

"Whatever," Dev grunted.

We turned past a dilapidated chicken coop, where, according to the sign, Sherman had once camped. Four horse paddocks and one old man on a tractor later, we arrived at Bentonville. The parking lot was packed with cars, and soldiers swarmed about the old white farmhouse and the seemingly endless series of enormous fields. Tall scrubby pines and green clinging vines framed the empty expanses of stubbly fields slowly filling with soldiers.

Beau went to join the rest of the men in the business of setting up the tents. I had business of my own to attend to. Dev wandered off, presumably to scope out the hottie situation. I crossed the field behind the farmhouse and waded into a sea of blue.

Garrett was easy to find. He was sitting on the fence that separated the battlefield from the registration area by the farmhouse, texting furiously into his cell phone.

"You shouldn't have that out, you know," I said.

"I'm on the fence." Garrett closed the phone and put it in his pocket. "It's fine on this side." He hopped off the fence, onto the side with the registration farmhouse.

"Still . . ." I shrugged. "You shouldn't."

"Finally decided to talk to me?" Garrett crossed his arms. "Or is this in your official capacity as historical accuracy police?"

"It's official. But not about that," I answered. "And you haven't exactly tried to talk to me either," I added in an undertone.

"Libby." He ran his hands over his face. "What the hell is going on with us? I don't understand why you keep avoiding me, why we're always fighting, why you ran away from me at that stupid Squirrel bar . . ."

"You don't understand?" My jaw fell open. "You are—you are unbelievable," I said, shaking my head. Of all the nerve! How dare he cheat on me and keep acting like he had no idea what was going on! I mean, I knew Garrett was smart, but I had thought crafty maliciousness like this was beyond him. And I sure hadn't known he was such a good actor.

"I just don't get it—"

"Whatever," I said, cutting him off. "I'll just do what I came here to do, and then I'm gone. Here." I shoved a fabric parcel at him.

"What the hell is this?" Garrett turned it over, squinting at it through his glasses.

"It was Corporal Anderson's jacket. Someone—or something—destroyed it," I said brusquely.

"Just because you like borrowing his clothes doesn't mean I do," Garrett muttered, and chucked the jacket into a patch of clinging vines.

"Hey!" I bent down to retrieve the jacket. "For your information—not that it even matters—Beau didn't even want me to give this to you! I only brought it because I thought you'd need it. For your story. If you're even working on the story anymore," I added. "Are you?" I asked searchingly. "Or are you too busy 'Skyping your editor' to do any work?"

The color drained from his face.

"Libby," he started. "I don't know what you think you—"

"Are you taking any of this seriously?" I continued. The words kept pouring out, and I couldn't stop them. "Why did you even come here, if you're just going to make fun of this and completely disrespect what you're supposed to be researching? You haven't committed to anything. I mean, you've made the most minimal concession possible to period clothing; you have your cell phone out in public; you're running off-site for coffee every five minutes—"

"Coffee? What?" he asked nervously.

"You're making no effort whatsoever to catch this ghost!" I shouted over him. "You're not spending any time in any of the places the ghost's been seen. You're not staking anything out. You didn't start sleeping over by the Fifteenth Alabama, like you said you would!"

"I couldn't!" Garrett exploded. "Libby, I couldn't. I couldn't spend time near him, with the way he so obviously likes you! And I'm not entirely sure you don't feel the same way!" He ran his hands through his hair, pulling on it like he always did when he was agitated. "I mean, is this what's going on? Would you rather be with him? Because . . . because I don't like playing dress-up, and I don't know who invented the teakettle, or whatever?"

"Really?" A strange, completely joyless laugh bubbled out of me. "Really? That's what you think is going on? That I have some sort of . . . crush? I would never, Garrett, I would never . . . Beau has nothing to do with this, nothing to do with us."

"I get it," he continued, still pulling at his hair. "Now I see what all this was about."

"What all what was about?" I countered.

"You—the way you've been acting."

"The way *I've* been acting?!" I said, shocked.

"Yeah, okay, Libby, you don't want to be with me, fine. But at least have the decency to end things with me before starting up with Johnny Redneck, okay?"

"I can't believe you—I can't—This has nothing to do with

me." I took a deep breath. "Garrett, I know. I *know.* Why can't you just *tell* me?"

"Tell you . . . what?" he asked, furrowing his brow.

"I can't—I can't even—I just can't," I sputtered, and let the torn jacket fall to the ground. I hopped over the fence and ran into the battlefield.

"Libby, come on!" Garrett yelled, as I disappeared into the field of blue soldiers, weaving through them and over to the gray side of the camp. "We need to talk about this! Whatever this is!"

I kept on running, and once I was sure I'd lost Garrett, I doubled back around to Sutlers' Row. I thought I spotted the now-familiar Dixie Acres tent, but that was the last thing I wanted to deal with right now.

"Runaway hooker!" Dev yelled, from inside our tent, which had been completely set up in my absence. "Are you trying to reenact some kind of Julia Roberts movie mash-up? *Runaway Bride* meets *Pretty Woman*?"

"No, I'm just trying to survive this hellhole," I said.

"You okay?" Dev squeezed my arm.

"I'm fine. Garrett and I just had a fight." I shook my head. "Let's just move some merch."

"That's my girl!" Dev clapped.

"Here's the last of it," said a tall, auburn-haired boy who entered holding a hatbox.

"Thanks, Beau—no, wait." I looked at him. He looked a lot like Beau, but it wasn't him.

"Naw, ma'am, I'm not Beau," he said, laughing as he set down the box. "I'm his cousin. Luke."

"Just like the Tarleton twins!" Dev whispered. "I told you there'd be two of them!"

"I'm with the Sixth Alabama Cavalry," Luke said, and saluted.

"Luke's been telling me *all* about riding those ponies." Dev almost purred.

Much to my surprise, Luke winked at him. Dev winked back. Well, at least someone's romantic future looked promising.

"Ma'am." Luke touched his hand to the brim of his cap. "Sir." He winked again, then walked out into the sunshine.

"Well, well, well." I shook my head. "I'm impressed. Look at you. Do you always get everything you want?" I teased.

"Oh, hush your mouth, Little Miss Thing." Dev swatted me away. "Go sell some skirts."

I obliged. The day passed slowly. I had no interest in the Battle of Bentonville raging outside; I could only think of the one I'd had with Garrett. How could he keep lying to me like that? To my face? Why wouldn't he just tell me what had happened?

We sold a lot of dresses, even more after Dev finally let me change—apparently my outfit was attracting too many husbands and not enough wives. I was more than happy to put on a more demure white lawn dimity number. When the battle ended at five, Luke stopped by to see if Dev wanted to "go walkin'."

"Libby," Dev said, with his patented puppy-dog eyes. "Do you mind if I—"

"Go." I shooed him along. "Go on, go. I've got everything covered."

"Merci, merci!" Dev sang as he skipped off with his man in uniform.

I spent the evening packing up products, itemizing receipts, and putting all the money in order. I borrowed a well-battered copy of *Uncle Tom's Cabin* from the canteen sutler next door and was all set to hunker down for a quiet night of reading by lamplight, when, several hours later, Dev burst through the tent.

"Come, come!" he said with a grin. "I have a surprise!"

"What?" I struggled up to sitting, fighting my petticoats. "What are you talking about?"

"Stand. Let me see," Dev ordered. "Not bad, not bad . . ." He popped open the trunk at the foot of his bed and pulled out some silk snowdrop flowers. After briskly putting up my hair, he pinned in the snowdrops. "Now we're ready."

He pulled me out of the tent.

"Where are we going?" I asked.

"Hi there, Libby." Luke was waiting outside the tent and joined us as we walked briskly away from the battlefield, into the woods.

"Uh, hi there, Luke," I said. "What's going on?" I asked Dev in an undertone. "Do you need a chaperone or something?"

"Of course not," he scoffed. "Libby, what's my philosophy on dating?"

"Men are like coffee," I recited. "The best ones are rich, hot, and can keep you up all night."

"No, no, my other philosophy. Although that is a good one," he amended. "The only way to get over someone is to get under someone else."

"Dev! Eeuw!"

"Sorry, sorry, pop back into your romantic fantasy bubble," he said, waving his hands. "Well, that shouldn't be too hard . . ."

He stopped and pointed.

"Oh my," I gasped. There was a small clearing in the woods illuminated by lamps hung in the trees. Garlands of silver fabric and ribbons also hung from the branches. Willie sat in a corner, a big pink bow tied around his neck. And directly in the center stood Beau, looking more handsome than ever. Even though he didn't have a jacket, he'd tied his officer's sash around his belt.

"Looks good, doesn't it?" Dev said proudly. "Luke and I may have helped with the practical details, but you should know, it was all soldier boy's idea." He nodded at Beau. "We'll leave you two to it."

Luke and Dev took hands and disappeared into the woods. Slowly, I walked into the glow of the lamplight.

"The Boone Hall Plantation Ball is next weekend," Beau said, as he stepped forward. "I figured we could use one more real good practice." He held out his hand. "May I have this dance?"

Wordlessly, I placed my hand in his. I heard a violin tuning up. Looking around, I noticed a small bald man playing a violin half hidden behind the tree.

"Behind the tree, Curly!" Dev hissed from somewhere in the darkness. "You're supposed to pretend you're not here, remember?!"

The man scuttled deeper into the woods.

"I'm sorry." Beau laughed. "I wanted this to be real special, but, well . . ." He shrugged. "It was the best I could do on short notice."

"It is special," I told him. I put my other hand on his shoulder, and he put his around my waist. "No one's ever done anything like this for me before."

"Well," Beau said, as we began to waltz, "I've never met anyone like you before."

I didn't know what to say to that, so all I did was dance.

"Is this"—I listened carefully—"is this a Taylor Swift song?"

I could hear Dev singing "Today Was a Fairytale" from inside a bush somewhere.

"It is!" I laughed.

"Well, I wouldn't know." Beau laughed along with me. "Blame my event coordinator. You're a sellout, Curly," he addressed the bald guy playing violin.

"What can I say? She writes songs with feeling!" Curly shot back from behind the tree.

We laughed and kept on dancing. I felt like I had never seen so many stars, had never felt like I could float before.

As the song slowed, so did we. Beau leaned down, closer and closer, and closed his eyes. A breath away from a kiss, I placed my hand on his chest and stopped him.

"Beau," I said, as his eyes fluttered open. "I'm sorry. I—I can't."

"All right." He nodded slowly. "I respect that. I understand. I'll wait."

"Beau, you don't have to wait . . . I mean I don't know when, or if I'll ever, or . . . I don't know . . ." I trailed off.

"I do," he said, taking a deep breath. "You and I both know the North should've won the war. Immediately. In a matter of weeks. Maybe less. They had all the advantages on their side.

But you know what the South had, Libby?" He picked up my hand and held it to his chest. "Heart. They fought harder and wanted it more. That's the only reason they hung on as long as they did. Heart."

"Oh, Beau, I—"

"So I'm gonna keep on hangin' on. Keep fighting. 'Cause that's the only thing I know how to do."

At that moment, a manic scream rent the night air. Beau and I sprung apart, as Willie howled along.

"That some kind of coyote or something?" Beau asked, scanning the woods.

"Nope, that's some kind of Dev. I'd recognize that shriek anywhere!" I cried. "He made the same noise when Lady Gaga's *The Fame* lost Album of the Year at the Grammys!" I started heading into the woods. "Come on! Let's go!"

Beau followed me. Dev was shivering in a bush less than twenty feet from the clearing.

"Libbbeeeee!" Dev shrieked. "It was back! She was back!"

"What? Who? She? The ghost?" I panicked. "Are you okay? Where's Luke?"

"He went after it!" Dev climbed out of the bush. "I was all 'Billy, don't be a hero, don't be a fool with your life,' but he just went after it!"

"Hell," Beau cursed. "I'm gonna go after him."

Before Beau could take off, Curly the violinist stumbled into our little area from behind his tree, followed closely by a rumbling Willie, and Luke jogged in from the other direction, holding a scrap of white fabric that glowed eerily in the moonlight.

"Did you get it?" Dev asked eagerly.

"Part of it." Luke held up the fabric scrap.

"All right, what exactly the hell happened here?" Beau crossed his arms.

"Well, we were having a lovely evening, dancing to 'Today Was a Fairytale,'" Dev began, "until this *thing* came along and ruined it!"

"She was streaking toward the camp," Luke continued. "She noticed us and seemed real interested in me. Started walkin' toward me real menacin' like."

"Probably 'cause she thought you were Beau," I supplied.

"Brill." Dev rolled his eyes.

"But then I started chargin' her," Luke said.

"You should've seen him—he was magnificent!" Dev jumped in.

"And wouldn't you know it, that thing just turned and ran! Real scared. I tried to get ahold of it, but it was a slippery little thing. And fast, too. I managed to get a piece of it, but it tore clean off, and the ghost got away."

The sound of twigs crashing and breaking interrupted Luke, as we all turned in the direction of the noise.

"Ghost!" Dev shrieked. Willie rushed to his side to protect him.

"We should be so lucky," I muttered, as a slightly out-of-breath Garrett thundered into the clearing.

"What the hell is going on?" Garrett said.

"What the hell are you doing here?" I said.

Garrett looked around at the assembled company, clearly bewildered.

"What is this, some kind of double date?" he asked.

"Yes, with a ghost and a bald violinist," I said, indicating Curly. "It's been very romantic," I added sarcastically. "Are you kidding?"

"Ghost?" Garrett said. "Wait, the ghost was here?"

"Emphasis on 'was,'" Dev said. "But she left behind a party favor."

Luke held it up. It shone in the moonlight.

"You know," I said, contemplating the fabric, "that looks awfully synthetic." I rubbed it between my fingers. "I'm pretty sure this is polyester . . . Dev?"

Dev took the scrap. He rubbed it. Sniffed it. Darted out his tongue to lick it. "Definitely polyester," he agreed.

"And the first polyester fiber wasn't created until 1941," I said. "So that can only mean one thing . . ."

"Zoinks!" Dev held the polyester up to the lantern light as Willie nuzzled closer to him. "That's no ghost, Scoobs. We've got ourselves a real live villain."

chapter eight

It was a full four-hour drive to Boone Hall Plantation, near Charleston, South Carolina. And there were no reenactments to stop at on the way, because pretty much all the major battles in South Carolina had been fought in or right near Charleston on the coast. So after a much-needed trucker shower, we careened, full steam ahead, farther and farther south, speeding past acres of trees where Spanish moss fell eerily between their branches. Everywhere we passed looked like a ghost town, and I couldn't help but feel like a ghost myself. Like I wasn't completely solid.

Dev had elected to ride with Luke to Boone Hall, which left me alone with Beau in the truck. Luckily, Willie had seen this as an opportunity to stretch out to his full length, resting his head contentedly in my lap as I played with his ears. I wasn't ready to sit too close to Beau. I wasn't sure if I'd ever be ready. We had come so close to kissing before the ghost interrupted things, and although I had stopped it, it still scared me how close we had gotten. We passed most of the drive in companionable silence as I drifted in and out of sleep, my dreams green and eerie, as if Spanish moss were hanging from the corners of my mind.

"Hey, now." A large, rough hand shook me gently. "You're gonna wanna wake up for this."

I blinked my eyes, waking up to a long road framed by a row of enormous oak trees dripping Spanish moss.

"Twelve Oaks," I whispered.

"Naw." Beau laughed softly. "This isn't *Gone with the Wind.* And we're not havin' a barbecue with Ashley Wilkes."

"But it looks just like it," I said, pointing out the window to the brick mansion with the giant white columns at the end of the alley of oaks.

"Twelve Oaks isn't real. Boone Hall Plantation was the inspiration for Twelve Oaks in *Gone with the Wind,* though," Beau explained. "This right here is one of the most iconic southern things you can see. Well, that and a fried green tomato, maybe. Only they're not much to look at."

"I can't imagine they're much to eat either," I said absent-mindedly, gazing with admiration at the beautiful house. It really was *Gone with the Wind* come to life. I'd never seen anything so elegant.

"None of that Yankee snobbery, please, miss," Beau admonished, as he turned away from the house and drove into an extensive parking lot already filling up with reenactors' cars. "Best damn things you'll ever eat, I promise you that. I'll have to get my mama to fry you up some. Next weekend, maybe. Although . . . wait . . ." He trailed off, suddenly realizing that our days were numbered.

"Summer's almost over," I mused, as I realized it too. "Crazy, isn't it? It went by so quickly. It feels like just yesterday your mom picked Dev and me up at the airport."

"A hell of a lot has happened, though," Beau replied, as he parked the car. "I mean, who ever heard of spendin' the summer with a ghost?"

"Well . . ." I said drily as I hopped out of the truck. Who ever heard of spending two summers with a ghost? Ridiculous.

"Don't think that'll bother us anymore, though," Beau said confidently, as he strode to the back of the truck. Willie clambered out of the truck and followed me around to join Beau. "Think Luke gave whatever it was a real scare. Haven't seen hide nor polyester hair of it since then, have we?"

"No, we have not," I agreed, as Beau began unloading things out of the truck bed.

"Knew all it needed was a good run at the thing, whatever it was. Why bother figurin' out what it was doin' there when you can just get rid of it?"

"Dunno," I muttered awkwardly, looking away, sidestepping that vague barb at Garrett. My eyes wandered to the front of the truck, where something that hadn't been there before was fluttering under a windshield wiper. "Beau, did you get a ticket?" I asked quizzically. "How could you get a parking ticket on a plantation?"

"Dunno. That's odd." He scratched his head under the brim of his kepi cap. "We just got here."

Beau hauled the last bag out of the truck, then we walked around to the front to see what it was.

"Not a parking ticket," I said, as Beau lifted it out from under the windshield wiper. It looked like some sort of old parchment, not like a ticket at all.

Beau scanned the note quickly. "Aw, hell," he muttered, then crumpled the paper and threw it to the ground.

"Hey!" I protested. "I wanted to read that!" I squatted awkwardly, my enormous skirts billowing about me, reaching forward to retrieve the note. Hastily, I uncrumpled it and read aloud: "Anderson: You've Been Warned." I looked up at Beau. "This—this looks like it was written in blood, too."

"We don't know that," he said stubbornly. "Might've just been a red pen or somethin'. Anyway, it doesn't matter anymore, does it?"

"How does it not matter?" I asked, rising and smoothing my skirts.

"Well, you and Dev figured it out. It's no ghost. Just some weird girl in a costume."

"That doesn't mean that whoever's doing this isn't dangerous!" I said somewhat shrilly, folding the note into neat, perfect quarters, with more force than necessary. "This . . . this woman, whoever she is, has targeted you from the beginning. She destroyed your jacket. Who knows what she'd do to you? Anyone who'd write notes in *blood* is clearly deranged!"

"Why, Libby." He stepped toward me, speaking softly. "You worried about me?"

"Of course I'm worried about you!" I threw my hands in the air. "You're being stalked by a psychopath! Frankly, I would've felt better if it were a ghost! A ghost can't hurt you!"

"You don't want me to get hurt?" He moved closer.

"Of—of course not," I stuttered.

"So you must care about me, at least a little," he said, his voice barely a whisper.

"Beau, I—"

"Oh, Libby." Beau sighed softly, pushing a curl off my face and tucking it gently behind my ear. "Give me somethin' to hope for."

He leaned in, slowly, and I watched him come closer. But before I put my hands up to stop him—

"What the hell!" Tires screeched, I heard a car door slam, and I jumped away from Beau, turning around. A frighteningly livid Garrett had parked next to us and was storming out of his car, right toward Beau. "Seriously, man, what the hell!"

"I'd appreciate it if you wouldn't use that kind of language in front of a lady," Beau said stiffly.

"Yeah, well I'd appreciate it if you and your bullshit southern chivalry backed the hell away from my girlfriend," Garrett shot back sarcastically.

"You lost the right to call her that," Beau replied, his accent thickening as he got increasingly upset.

"Garrett—" I started.

"Really, Libby?" Garrett turned to face me. "This is how you end it? Letting Bo Duke feel you up next to the General Lee?"

"How dare you talk to her like that!" Beau interrupted. "Considerin' how—how—deplorably you've conducted yourself."

"What the hell are you talking about, Jethro Bodine?" Garrett said snidely.

"Hannah," I whispered. Both men immediately silenced and turned to face me. Garrett looked paler than I'd ever seen him; he was nearly translucent. "I saw you with her," I said softly. "I know, Garrett. I saw you kiss her."

An excruciatingly long silence descended on the three of us.

"I'll, uh, leave you two to it," Beau muttered quietly, and walked off toward the reenactment.

"How did—I don't understand—I—I didn't," Garrett said finally, shaking his head. "Libby, what?"

I sighed heavily. "Dev and I took Beau's truck. Because he wanted coffee."

"Starbucks," Garrett said quietly.

"Starbucks," I confirmed. "We saw you through the window. We saw the two of you together. We saw you—"

"Hug her," he said firmly. "That was all that happened. I didn't kiss her. I would never, Libby, never. I swear."

"Why did you even see her?" I whispered, blinking back tears. "And why didn't you tell me?"

"Well, she—she's doing a summer internship at Duke."

"I know," I said.

"You know?" he asked.

"Um—never mind," I said quickly. "Long story. Go on."

"Well, she saw on Facebook that I was in North Carolina—"

"You're still Facebook friends?!" I burst out. "Really? She *cheated* on you, and you didn't defriend her?!" Garrett shot me a look. "Sorry, not the point right now. Keep going."

"Anyway, she messaged me. Said she wanted to talk about what happened. Apologize. That she felt really bad about the way she'd treated me. That she'd feel a lot better if we could talk."

"And you went?"

"I don't know, Libby—I felt bad!" He ran his hands through his hair. "Honestly, I thought it might make me feel better too. I was still so angry at her. Still hurt. I thought it might help . . . lessen that."

"Oh," I said in a small voice. "Did it?"

"Actually, yeah." He nodded. "It did. The hug was just a hug. Nothing more. An 'I'm sorry, I forgive you' kind of deal. That was it. And now it really feels over."

"And you didn't tell me—"

"I didn't tell you because it didn't matter. She doesn't matter to me anymore."

"I'm so relieved." I smiled, and squeezed his hand. "It was just a misunderstanding. Just like you thought Beau and I—"

He shook my hand off, scowling. "I don't think I misunderstood anything," Garrett said darkly.

"Wait—what?" I gasped.

"You heard me," he said tersely.

"Don't you see how unfair you're being?" I cried. "If I can believe you, you should be able to believe me!"

"I've seen the way he looks at you," he said quietly. "And even worse, I've seen the way you look at him."

"Garrett, stop, you're being ridiculous—"

"I'm not," he said, anger darkening the edges of his voice. "There are parts of you he understands in a way I never will. He's part of this fantasy world you want so badly to be a part of, a world I have no interest in belonging to."

"You could be a part of it too," I said tentatively. "Maybe—maybe you could come to the ball tomorrow night?"

"Come to the ball?" He laughed hollowly. "Are you kidding? This place . . . this place is disgusting."

"What are you talking about?" I shook my head in disbelief. "This place is stunning." I gestured to the mansion. "Look at it!"

"Come with me," he barked, then turned on his heels and started walking briskly toward the back of the house. I followed, trotting on my impractical heels, trying to keep up.

"Look," Garrett announced, when we arrived in back of the mansion to face rows and rows of tiny, poorly constructed brown cabins. They were little better than shacks.

"Are these the slave quarters?" I asked quietly.

"This is what built everything 'stunning' you see out there," he said somberly. "Didn't even notice, did you?" He pointed to the row of cabins. "Bet you had no idea this was back here."

"I just got here!" I protested.

"See, Libby? It's fake. Everything here is fake. This is the reality—people suffering, in shitty, crumbling cabins. That big, glamorous façade out there is just that. A façade. It's not real, Libby." He ran his hands through his messy hair. "Nothing here is real."

"It's just a dance, Garrett," I said shakily.

"Is it?"

I took a deep breath. "Yes, it is. A dance. Just a dance." I took his hand. "Where I want to dance with you."

"I don't want any part of that," he said, wriggling away. "You want the perfect façade—he's right out there waiting for you."

"Maybe you're right." I stepped away. "You don't understand me. At all."

Fighting back tears, I turned, picked up my skirts, and ran, away from him, back to the big house, where things were far less complicated. *I will not cry,* I told myself silently, breathing deeply. *I will not cry.*

By the time I reached the field, all of the tents were set up. I spotted ours easily, the Confederate Couture sign twinkling in the evening light out front.

"Helloooo!" Dev chirped as I poked my head into the tent. He and Luke were sitting on Dev's cot in our tent, their laps full of yarn. "I'm teaching Luke how to crochet!" Grinning, the two of them held up their needles to display identical partially completed socks.

"Could the two of you please be a little less cute right now?" I complained good-naturedly. They exchanged glances.

"Man troubles, darlin'?" Luke said seriously, setting down his sock. "You decided to let that cousin of mine sweep you off your feet yet?"

"You thrown that rat bastard out on his ass yet?" Dev flung his sock aside.

"Still not sure, and, well, it's over." I plunked down on my cot.

Luke made a sympathetic clucking noise with his tongue.

"About damn time," Dev muttered. Luke elbowed him in the ribs. "I mean"—Dev rested his chin on his hand—"how are you feeling?"

"Fine, fine, I'll be fine." I flopped back on the cot, resting my head on my thin pillow. "Carry on with your crocheting."

"Well, tomorrow you'll be more than fine," Dev sang out gaily, "as in 'damn fine.' As in 'Damn, guuuuurl, you fine!'"

"What are you talking about?" I rolled over to face the crocheting couple.

"Ball tomorrow!" Dev scolded. "Where's your head at?"

"Head's on a pillow." I rolled back over. "Going to sleep."

"Um, it's like mad early—"

"Going to sleep," I repeated.

Despite the fact that it was, as Dev had pointed out, "mad early," and despite the fact that I was still fully clothed and corseted, I fell asleep. I woke up the next morning feeling like I was inside a strange, clouded fog. Were Garrett and I really not together anymore? How was that possible? I rolled over and went back to sleep, desperate to shut out reality.

And yet, somehow, hours later, I was standing in the middle of our tent, clad in silks and satins.

"Who else has a fairy godmother who just keeps on

improving?!" Dev patted himself on the back. "Hellooooo, Cinderella! Stunning!" He twittered around me like an excited sparrow, picking and fussing and fixing and straightening.

I didn't care what I looked like. I was sure the dress looked beautiful, because it was a stunning dress. It was a shade of blue so pale it was nearly a silvery white, and it shimmered when it caught the light. The low-cut neckline was trimmed with unbelievably intricate lace, and the skirt ballooned around me in a perfect arc. I had agreed to five petticoats for tonight.

"Smile, honey," Dev commanded as he pinned silver silk flowers into my hair. "There. You're perfect."

I wasn't perfect. I would never be perfect. And I was starting to realize that perfect might have been the last thing I wanted to be.

I had been looking forward to the Boone Hall Plantation Ball all summer, but now that it was here, I couldn't have cared less. All I could think about was the one person who wouldn't be going to the ball. Was he telling the truth? I wanted to believe him, but I was scared. And I was telling the truth, but it didn't seem possible for him to believe me.

"Hello!" Dev snapped his fingers in front of my face. "The boys will be here in, like, two seconds. Stop zoning out!"

As if Dev had summoned them, a sweet southern drawl called out, "Are y'all ready, or what?"

"Luke, you should've knocked, not hollered at 'em," Beau reprimanded.

"Knock on what? It's a tent!"

"Keep your trousers on, boys, we're coming!" Dev yelled back. "Oops, wait, fan." He shoved a white lace fan into my fingerless-gloved hands, pulled the tent flap back with a flourish, and pushed me through.

"Holy-Mary-mother-of-God," Beau whispered, all in one breath. At his heels, Willie barked twice. He seemed to approve.

"Has the South risen again?" Dev smirked.

"Hush, you." Luke rapped his knuckles. "Behave. There's a lady present."

"You look . . . stunning," Beau said, as he walked toward me and picked up one fingerless-gloved hand. "You sure stunned me." He bent to kiss my hand through the white net lace, eyes locked with mine as his lips lingered on the back of my hand.

"Um, hello, have I not stunned anyone?" Dev demanded, hands on the hips of his perfectly tailored black suit, jacket with tails open to reveal a pale blue silk jacquard brocade vest and a giant white floppy cravat.

"You stunned me the minute you walked into my life in that devastatin' mornin' frock coat," Luke said mistily, enveloping Dev in a giant bear hug and holding him close.

"Wrinkles!" Dev shrieked, wriggling away. "Don't wrinkle the suit!" Luke rolled his eyes good-naturedly, leaned in, and kissed him on the cheek. "Much better." Dev patted Luke fondly. "You can wrinkle me all up after the ball," he added cheekily.

"All right, Martha Stewart, let's get you in there wrinkle-free," Luke said, taking Dev's hand. "Shall we?"

Beau still had my hand. He squeezed it gently, and we followed Dev and Luke away from Sutlers' Row and toward the mansion, with Willie trotting along behind us. When we got there, however, it looked like a bunch of gophers had beat us to it. The lawn had been torn up, and soldiers with shovels were hastily trying to beat it back into submission.

"Um, eeuw, who was in charge of the landscaping for this event?" Dev shuddered. "This is heinous. What is the theme here, early World War I trenches?"

"Naw, they had a bit of a problem earlier with Ol' Spookie." Luke chuckled. "Had to get her last warnin' in—"

"Luke," Beau warned.

"What's going on?" I clued in to the conversation for the first time. "The ghost is back? What did she do? And what did it have to do with the lawn?"

"Easy there, Nancy Drew," Dev muttered.

"Nothin', really," Beau said, patting my arm. "Really nothin' to get worried about at all. Nothin' to worry anyone about." He looked meaningfully at Luke.

"Yeah, Ol' Spookie just tore up part of the ground with a shovel, jes' like some kid playin' in the sand, writin' out a message—"

"What did it say?" I asked sharply.

"I come for you tonight," Luke answered in an eerie tone.

"Luke!" Beau warned again, more forcefully this time.

"Aw, come on, cuz, she's a big girl; she can handle it." Luke shrugged nonchalantly. "Doesn't matter. Jes' some idiot playin' in the dirt."

"Exactly. It doesn't matter," Beau said firmly.

"Doesn't matter? She's coming for you! Tonight!" I said, my voice getting increasingly shrill.

"And she's a crazy bitch with a shovel!" Dev added gleefully.

"Libby, really, it's nothin' to worry about." Beau squeezed

my arm. "Let's just enjoy the ball, all right? Hey, now, look over there."

I followed his gaze to a small tent just off to the side of the mansion with a small group of people clustered around it. Blinding flashes of light emitted from it at sporadic intervals.

"OMG, is that a paparazzi station?! Like at a red carpet event?!" Dev started bouncing up and down, clutching at Luke's arm. "Can we go? Can we? Can we?!"

"Kind of," Beau explained, as we moved closer to the tent. "They've got a really well-done replica of a camera from the 1860s in there, and they're takin' photographs. Just like Mathew Brady."

"'I'm your biggest fan, I'll follow you until you love me,'" Dev sang, completely off-key as always.

"Darlin', please don't butcher the Lady." Luke winced, covering his ears, as Willie whined before collapsing to roll around in the grass.

Dev stuck his tongue out at Luke as the four of us waited in line at the photography tent. Once it was our turn, Luke and Dev scampered up first, Dev flinging his arms up to pose in front of his handsome boy in uniform. The photographer raised an eyebrow but said nothing before disappearing under the black cloth to take their picture. Luke pulled a reluctant Dev out of the spotlight, and Beau gently led me into the center of the tent.

"What a perfect couple." Dev sighed, clutching Luke's arm with glee. "Doesn't she look beautiful! Libby, you look so beautiful!"

I didn't feel beautiful. I didn't feel anything. I was empty.

Hollow. Numb. A beautiful glass bubble. I painted on my smile and stared vacantly out at the photographer. I could feel heat radiating from Beau's arm where my hand rested elegantly on his jacket, but it didn't reach me. I was cold all the way through.

Light exploded with a blinding flash.

"You all right?" Beau patted my white-gloved hand with his. "You don't seem quite yourself tonight."

"Oh, I'm fine," I reassured him. "Just fine." I squeezed his arm and smiled shakily as we walked up toward the house. Willie stopped his rolling and jumped up to follow us in.

"Stay here," Beau ordered Willie, once we'd climbed the steps of the porch and our canine companion showed no sign of abandoning us. Willie whined in response. "I mean it, now," he said more firmly. Willie whined one more time, then resigned himself to his fate, lying down on the porch and resting his head on his paws. "Good boy." Beau scratched his ears. "Shall we?"

Beau led me inside. It was stunning. The barbecue at Twelve Oaks didn't hold a candle to this shimmering golden whirl of Technicolor silks and satins. Soldiers in blue and gray mingled, laughing, the war put on hold for tonight.

"I think I've died and gone to taffeta heaven!" Dev pretended to swoon. "Where can a nice boy like me get a drink in a place like this? Take me to the punch, soldier!"

Dev and Luke disappeared into the world of whirling couples.

"Well, Libby," Beau said, turning to face me, as the couples applauded the end of a dance. "It's what we've been waiting for." He bowed while the orchestra tuned up for what sounded like the beginning of a waltz. "I think they're playing our song." He grinned and held out his hand.

I took his hand, and he led me into the center of the floor, pulling me into him, his hand warm and strong on the small of my back. As the orchestra began to play—a waltz, just as I'd thought—he steered me around the room with easy confidence. But despite the fact that Beau was dancing beautifully, that even I was dancing beautifully for once, I couldn't stop searching for a familiarly awkward, lanky frame. Every time I spotted the top of a brown, curly head, I looked for glasses, but it wasn't him. He wasn't coming. He was never coming.

"Air," I said. "I think I need some air." The dance had stopped, but the couples hadn't stopped spinning. The room wouldn't stop spinning. What had I done? Had I really lost Garrett? And what was I doing here, in this room, in this place where nothing was real, dancing like nothing mattered, while I was losing the person who mattered most to me? Losing something real?

"I knew you weren't all right." Beau grabbed me by both shoulders, steadying me on my swaying feet. "How 'bout a cold drink? I'm gonna get you a lemonade. A lemonade, all right?" I nodded mutely. "Head out onto the terrace and get some air. I'll be there in a minute."

Nodding, I walked shakily toward the back of the ballroom, toward the terrace, the cool night air pulling me onward like a beacon. It was completely empty out there, and I clung to a wrought-iron railing, shining in the Carolina moonlight. Beau returned mere moments later, clutching a glass of lemonade like a life raft.

"Here you go." He held out the cup, and I took a small sip.

"Libby, tell me. What's going on?" he asked searchingly, his eyes locking with mine. "Is there somethin' I can do?"

"No." I shook my head, setting my lemonade down on a curve of the banister. "No, there's nothing you can do. Nothing more, I mean. Because you're perfect." I paused, taking a deep breath. "But I'm not looking for perfect. I'm looking for the opposite, actually. I'm looking for real. And that's the opposite of what this is. Because none of this is real. Not even . . . us, I don't think."

"Libby," he said, taking my hands. "Just 'cause I'm not wearin' my Crimson Tide T-shirt and you're not wearin' jeans, doesn't mean what we have isn't real."

"I think it does." I sighed. "It's like . . . It's like . . . *The Bachelor,* or something. You think you feel something, because you're in this magical world, where everything's perfect, with fantasy dates and helicopters and hot tubs—"

"Or horseshit and hardtack," Beau interrupted. "Crazy romantic."

"I'm being serious." I kept going. "This can't be real, because this world isn't real. I don't think we'd work outside of it. Just like nobody on *The Bachelor* stays together."

"Trista and Ryan," Beau said stubbornly. "So did Jason and Molly."

"I am . . . stunned that you know that," I said, my jaw dropping.

"My mama watches it." He shrugged sheepishly.

"Jason and Molly aside," I continued. "You're wonderful. But the problem is, no matter how wonderful you are, you're not—not—"

"Not him," Beau finished for me.

"I'm in love with somebody else," I whispered.

"And no amount of horseshit and hardtack is gonna change that," he murmured.

"Oh, Beau—"

"I don't think I can stop loving you." He dropped my hands. "But I can let you go. Because I know that's the right thing to do."

"Beau." I leaned up to kiss him on the cheek. "I'm so sorry. And thank you. And—"

"Go, Libby." He smiled sadly. "Just go."

Giving him one last look, I picked up my enormous skirts and ran down the steps of the terrace, into the gardens in back of the house. I sped through lanes and hedgerows, past roses and fountains, thinking only that I had to find Garrett. Had to fix this. Fix us. Only where would I find him? In his tent at the Union camp, probably.

A familiar bark interrupted my thoughts. A hundred pounds of dog was joyously romping behind me. He must have been wandering around outside the ball trying to find someone to cuddle.

"Oh, Willie, stop!" I yelled back at him as he kept barking. "Stay! I mean shoo! I mean, go back to the porch!" Willie kept following me, tongue lolling gaily out of his mouth. "Oh, for Pete's sake," I muttered, and picked up speed, wheezing in my corset. Willie kept pace.

The formal gardens ended, and I was through the garden gate and into the slave quarters. The crumbling little cabins looked even creepier at night. All I had to do was make it through the slave quarters, and then I was pretty sure the Union tents would appear.

Until an eerie white figure that most definitely did not belong back there appeared several hundred feet in front of us.

"Oh, no," I whispered, as I skidded to a halt, kicking up dirt with my satin dress slippers as the ghostly white psycho stood in front of me. "Oh, no, no, no."

Willie, unfortunately, had the opposite response. He barked joyously, did a little hop, then leaped forward, full steam ahead, racing toward another playmate.

"No, Willie!" I shouted. "No! No! Bad dog! Come here!"

My calls unheeded, I started chasing Willie. I mean, who knew what this woman would do to a poor defenseless dog? I was pretty sure she'd killed those chickens. Maybe she would do something terrible with dog blood! And it was Beau's dog. Who knew what sort of terrible vengeance she'd wreak on his poor innocent puppy?

Unless . . . unless *she* didn't actually come up with any of this stuff. Maybe she was just following someone else's orders. Someone who would have done anything to start getting soldiers off the battlefield so he could start building his precious housing development. . . . Realization hit me like a thunderclap. Was it possible the ghost was the Mrs. America Southern belle from Dixie Acres?

Willie, not wearing a corset, was much faster than I was and leaped right on top of the ghost before I had a chance to stop him. I heard a loud, high-pitched scream, then realized that I had been the one who screamed.

The ghost fell to the ground like a sack of potatoes, with Willie standing on top of her, licking her face.

"Willie!" I cried, and sped toward him.

"Aw, hell, get off!" shouted a voice that was definitely not female. Now I was confused. "I can't move! Get this stupid thing offa me! How the hell much does this damn dog weigh?"

By the time I'd gotten close enough to lean in and see who it was, Willie had licked off all of his makeup.

"Cody?!" I asked incredulously, leaning in to peer closer. "Is that you?"

"Aw, hell, Libby?" Cody sat up slightly as Willie started licking the white makeup off his arms. "Of all the people I didn't want to see me like this." He pulled off his wig and stared glumly at it.

I heard a sound behind us. I looked up, and people had started to pour out of the mansion. I thought I recognized Luke, Dev, and Captain Cauldwell at the front of the crowd.

"You are in very big trouble, young man," I said imperiously, hands on my hips.

"Don't I know it," he muttered.

"Libby!" I looked to my left, and my heart skipped a beat as a tall, uncoordinated someone thrashed his way awkwardly out of the woods. Garrett burst through the trees into the alley of slave quarters, panting. "Are you all right? What happened? I heard you scream! You really do have impressive projection. Must be the singing, right? I . . ." He trailed off, as he looked down and caught sight of Willie and Cody on the ground. "Oh. Um. My. Well. Look at that. You caught the ghost."

"Actually, Willie caught the ghost." I shrugged.

"Is that . . ." Garrett swooped down to peer into Cody's face. "The Boy Scout? The pervy one?"

"Aw, shut it," Cody said, swatting him away. Willie jumped back on top of him, knocking him flat on the ground. "Ouch!" Cody shrieked.

By this time, the crowd had caught up with us. It looked like every single person who had been at the ball had spilled out of the house and was now clustered around Cody.

"You all right?" Beau reached me first. "Was that you who screamed?" I could feel Beau and Garrett sizing each other up behind me. "He try to hurt you?"

"What? What, no, of course not!" I turned to Beau. "It's—"

"Ghost!" Dev shrieked. "Oh, no, wait a minute . . . Oh, no, it can't be . . . O . . . M . . . G . . ." Dev leaned closer and closer, until he lifted up one of Willie's floppy ears to peer underneath. "It's the tiny gremlin!"

"Cody?!" Beau asked incredulously.

"Son, what in the hell do you think you're doin'?!" Captain Cauldwell thundered.

"The tiny gremlin's a tranny!" Dev cackled. "Oooh, oooh, I have a front-page headline! Garrett, Garrett, listen to this!" He hopped over to Garrett. "'Transvestite Tot Terrorizes Tiny Towns!' No! Wait! 'Drag Queen Teen in Spooky Scene!' Eh? Eh? I'm the one who should be writing for the paper!"

"I'll think about it, Dev," Garrett said equitably as he whipped out his cell phone and started snapping pictures of Cody.

"Cody, why did you do it?" Beau asked, somewhat bewildered. "Did I—Did I do somethin' wrong?"

"Naw, not really. Sort of." Cody struggled to a sitting position, as Beau helped pull Willie off. "It's not just you. It's all of this." He gestured vaguely to the house, the grounds, all the people clustered about. "It's a waste of a summer, marchin' around like a dumbass in the heat, when I coulda been hangin' out with my friends, instead of stuck here with you rejects."

"So what was the plan?" Garrett swooped in, voice recorder in hand, gearing into reporter mode. "Scare a few kids, hope the whole thing'd get shut down, and you'd be sent home to Montgomery?"

"Pretty much," Cody grumbled. "I jes' wanted to get the hell out of here. An' I figured if enough Boy Scouts went home, they'd shut down the whole program altogether. An' I could go home without gettin' in any kind of trouble."

"Unluckily for you," Randall said, pushing his pale, pointed face to the front of the crowd, "we Boy Scouts are made of stronger mettle. Except for you, that is," he sniffed.

"Why Corporal Anderson?" Garrett pressed on. "Personal grudge?"

"He's a pain in the ass," Cody grumbled. "Ol' Stick-Up-His-Butt Anderson. Too much damn enthusiasm for this whole mess. Then he starts movin' in on my woman—"

Both Beau and Garrett shifted uncomfortably.

"Weren't there ghost rumors even before I got here?" I jumped in quickly, trying to break the tension.

"Sure, sure." Cody shrugged. "I Googled ghost stories, and, shit, wouldn't you know, that whole Anderson business popped right up. It was damn easy. Gave me a built-in motivation for hauntin' this stupid regiment."

"And the dress was just an added bonus?" Dev quipped.

"No way!" Cody shrieked. "I had to! It was the only thing that made sense! And the best way to mess with stupid Corporal Anderson! And—and—"

"And you would have gotten away with it, if it weren't for us meddling kids?" Dev cut him off, a twinkle in his eyes.

"What the hell you talking about, Gramps?" Cody snarled.

"And, of course, a pup named Scooby-Doo!" Dev cheered. Willie whined. "Er, I mean Willie," Dev corrected himself.

"Son, you're comin' with me," Captain Cauldwell ordered. Clamping a firm hand on Cody's shoulder, Captain Cauldwell picked him up and led him back to the house. Willie followed, still trying to lick the makeup off his legs. Dev, giggling gleefully, stayed as close to Cody as possible, dragging Luke behind him.

Cody. Huh. I had been so sure it was Cheyenne! The Dixie Acres guy had such a good motivation for getting rid of us. I wondered where they were tonight. Well, commotion or not, they didn't ever seem to be permitted onto the historical property.

Gradually, the rest of the crowd dispersed, until only Beau, Garrett, and I remained.

"You found him, then?" Beau asked, awkwardly shuffling at the ground. "And you're okay?" I nodded. He nodded in return. "All right, then, I'll, uh, leave you to it." He turned to go. "Holler if you need me," he said, before slowly walking back toward the mansion.

"You were looking for me?" Garrett furrowed his brow. "At the ball? Or, uh, outside of the ball? Is that why you came out here? Alone? In the dark?" He was talking faster and faster. "Libby, who knows what was out here? Is out here? What if that hadn't been Cody? What if—"

"I'm fine, Garrett." I shushed him. "But are we fine?"

"Oh." He reddened and scuffed his foot in the dirt. "Oh, I don't—I don't know. Do you want us to be fine?" He looked up at me.

"I do. I want us to be fine," I said tentatively.

"I do too," he blurted out in a rush. "But Beau . . . and you —I'm just not sure—"

"Garrett." I sighed heavily, taking his hands. "I want to be with you. But I need to be with someone who trusts me. And I want you to be that someone. But I don't know if you can."

"I want to be," he said, nodding earnestly. "I really, really want to be that someone."

"I know." I shook my head sadly and wrapped my arms around him. "You can trust me," I whispered. "Always." He remained stiff in my arms, but I could feel him reach one hand up to stroke my hair. I pulled away gently. "Think about it. If you can be that someone"—I leaned up to kiss him on the cheek—"let me know."

My head held high, I made my way out of the slave quarters, through the garden, and over to my tent on Sutlers' Row. I wanted to be with him, more than I wanted almost anything, but if he couldn't trust me, then I knew it wouldn't work.

The tent was empty, as Luke and Dev were still presumably watching the Cody drama unfold or dancing the night away. I fell into a dreamless sleep, and before I knew it, another morning was dawning, bringing another battle, and a sight that had never before been seen inside the Colonial Couture tent.

"This is a cruel and unusual punishment," Cody moaned.

"You wanted to wear a dress so bad, you got it!" Dev cackled. "If you can't do the time, don't do the crime. Ever heard the phrase 'the crime fits the punishment,' tiny gremlin? You perpetrated a cruel and unusual crime."

As part of the first phase of his punishment, Dev had requisitioned Cody as a human mannequin. He was currently standing on a box in front of the Colonial Couture tent, dressed in the frilliest dress and bonnet Dev could find.

"Can I at least get some water? This is inhumane."

Calmly, Dev picked up a dipper full of water from the bucket outside our tent and flung it full in Cody's face. Dripping, Cody screeched and spluttered.

"Careful, dear." Dev returned the dipper to the bucket. "Mannequins should be seen and not heard."

I laughed, for what felt like the first time in a long while. I still hadn't heard from Garrett. I mean, it's not like I expected him to burst into my tent with a bouquet of roses belting out "Endless Love" or something.

"I can't believe this is the last battle of the summer," I mused.

"I know, weirdsies, right?" Dev rummaged around in the boxes behind the racks in the tent, extracting his telescope. "Hence the extra-special outfits." He used the telescope to point at me.

"Um, yeah, about that," I said, looking down at my dress, which was an exact replica of Scarlett O'Hara's Twelve Oaks barbecue dress. But in pink. "I'm not sure this is accurate . . ."

"Accurate, schmaccurate. If you're not going to bust out the pink suit on the last day, when can you?" He was, in fact, wearing a pink suit.

"YOU!"

A male voice boomed out as Dev and I swiveled to see who it was. A livid man dressed in khakis and a pink polo shirt was barreling toward us, a stack of newspapers under his arm, trailed by a tall blonde in a zebra-print halter dress tripping over the uneven ground in sky-high heels.

"You owe me several million dollars, you uppity Yankee bitch!" he snarled.

"Watch it," Dev warned him. "Or I'll teach you the meaning of the word 'bitch.'" He flexed his slender muscles in a menacing manner. Or a manner intended to be menacing, at least.

"What are you talking about?" I asked nervously. I finally recognized him as the Dixie Acres guy—he just wasn't wearing a suit. And that must have been Cheyenne, liberated from her peach Southern belle get-up.

"You killed my development!" he bellowed. "I don't know how you did it, but I know it was you! Anything you care to tell me about this?" He threw the stack of newspapers onto the table that held our cash box. Curious, Dev and I started rifling through them. *Tuscaloosa News. Mobile Press-Register. Huntsville Times. Birmingham News. Atlanta Journal-Constitution.* And at the very bottom of the stack, a well-traveled-looking *Boston Globe.* Dev flicked through the *Tuscaloosa News* until he found an article entitled "A Second Civil War: The Fight for History."

"Every damn newspaper, the same damn appeal. For *help.* To save some stupid piece of chicken-shit cow pasture I was gonna *save* through economic redevelopment!"

"People gave money?" I asked. I skimmed the article. It was exactly that: an appeal for money to save the battlefields that Dixie Acres planned to build on, and a denunciation of Dixie Acres in general.

"Don't play stupid. Enough money poured in to create a private trust to protect the main plots of land I was gonna buy. And worse than that, no one'll touch any of my condos with a ten-foot pole! The whole thing is sunk. How the hell did a little idiot like you pull that off?"

"How indeed would such a story travel all the way to Boston?" Dev asked drily, finger tapping against the article's byline.

And there it was, in black-and-white: Garrett McCaffrey. Garrett had single-handedly saved dozens of Southern battlefields from destruction and Dixie Acres. For someone who claimed to be not interested in history, he had accomplished one of the most impressive feats of preservation in the last decade.

I turned to face Mr. Dixie Acres.

"I wish I could take credit for this, but I can't," I said in a strong, clear voice. "But I couldn't be happier that it happened. Now, unless you're interested in purchasing some Confederate Couture, I suggest you leave the tent. Before our guard-mannequin forcibly evicts you."

Dev gave me the thumbs-up, and even Cody, miserable in his frilly bonnet, nodded approvingly. Muttering menacingly, Mr. Dixie Acres stormed away, followed by his erstwhile Southern belle. I grinned as they retreated.

"Well, that sure beats flowers." Dev chuckled. "Here, honey, I got you this bouquet of protected battlefields."

"I can't believe it." I shook my head. "That is the most wonderful, most amazing—I just—I just can't believe." I had quite literally been stunned speechless.

"Unbelievable," Dev agreed, raising the telescope to his eye.

"What are you doing?" I asked absent-mindedly, privately counting down the minutes until the battle was over and I could find Garrett.

"Looking for my man on the battlefield. And whatever hotties might catch my eye."

"You're terrible." I shook my head, grinning.

"Let's see . . . starting with the boys in blue . . ." Dev appraised the field, calling out rankings as he looked over different soldiers. "Fug, fug, decent, jailbait, hairy, average, average plus, ugh, no, not hot, *and* wearing farby glasses . . ."

"Farby glasses?" I interrupted. "Someone's wearing historically inaccurate glasses?"

"Yeah, looks like they have plastic frames." Dev squinted through the lens.

"Oh my God," I said.

"Oh my God," Dev said.

"What?" we said simultaneously.

"It has to be Garrett, right?" I asked hopefully. "I mean, it has to. Who else would wear plastic-framed glasses into battle?"

"'The Second Vermont Brigade: Sponsored by Green Mountain Coffee,'" Dev read with wonderment.

"He's marching into battle, even though he thinks reenactments are stupid." I clutched Dev's arm, my heart pounding. "He saved dozens of battlefields, *and* he's participating in a historical activity! This has to mean something, right? Doesn't it have to?"

"This is real coffee, Libby," Dev said, putting the telescope down to face me. "One hundred percent arabica coffee."

We smiled at each other.

"You go get your coffee," I said.

"And you go get your man," he replied.

Leaving Cody sweating in the sun in his frilly dress, we

sprinted away. Dev ran through Sutlers' Row, taking the quickest route to the coffee. I, however, plunged headlong into the midst of the battle. I mean, how else was I supposed to find him?

I ran through the ranks, sidestepping horses, coughing as guns discharged around me, filling the air with thick gray smoke.

"It appears we have a civilian on the field," the commentator boomed over the loudspeakers. Oh. Whoops. "She appears to be a short blonde dressed head to toe in pink." Well, at least now, Garrett probably knew I was looking for him.

A cannon exploded behind me. I ducked, instinctually, even though I knew there weren't real cannonballs in it.

"You crazy, lady?" I heard a man shout behind me. "Get off the field!"

I ignored him and kept on running, through the cloud of cannon smoke, lifting my skirts to jump over bodies in the field, weaving my way through ranks of blue and gray.

Finally, I spotted the telltale plastic glasses glinting in the sun.

"Garrett!" I called, completely out of breath from running in a corset, resting my hands on my knees as I tried to catch my breath. "What are you doing?"

"Libby!" he shouted back, and pushed his way out of formation to join me. It was really Garrett, dressed in full Union uniform. "What are *you* doing?"

"Oh, you know, just out for a run," I joked, wheezing. "Seriously. What are you doing?"

"Trying to be a part of your world." He slung his rifle over his shoulder. "If this is important to you, then it's important to me too. Because you're important to me. More important than anything."

"Oh, Garrett." I straightened up to look at him. "You didn't have to do this—"

"I know," he interrupted me. "I wanted to. I really, really wanted to. I want to be that someone for you. Because I do trust you, Libby," he said, taking my hands. "This doesn't excuse the way I treated you. But . . . I was scared. Scared of getting hurt again and, worst of all, scared of losing you."

"You're not going to lose me." I squeezed his hands. "And I would never, never hurt you."

"I know," he said, pulling me into his arms, and finally everything felt right again. "I'm so sorry, Libby. But I mean . . . I'm only human," he whispered in my ear. "And you're Wonder Woman."

"You're superhuman, Garrett," I interrupted him. "What you did was . . . extraordinary. With your article in all those newspapers, I mean. Saving all those battlefields? That was incredible."

"It was the right thing to do." He blushed. "And I knew it was important to you."

"You're what's important to me," I said, smiling. "Losing you would be a million times worse than losing any battlefield."

"Even Gettysburg?"

I nodded.

"Okay, now you're just trying to butter me up," he said, and chuckled.

"There's no part of the past I would trade for my future with you," I said seriously.

I rose up on my tiptoes, threw my arms around his neck, and kissed him.

I could still hear cannons exploding around us. But I knew the war was over.

suggestions for further reading

Libby here! I learned a lot about the Civil War this summer, but there is SO much more cool stuff out there about this super-interesting chapter in American history. I just *had* to give you a few more suggestions . . . Have fun nerding out!

The Civil War: A Narrative, by Shelby Foote

Seriously everything you ever needed to know about the Civil War. It's long, but don't be intimidated—it's super good, I promise!

Gettysburg, by Stephen W. Sears

The ultimate book about the ultimate battle.

The Republic of Suffering: Death and the American Civil War, by Drew Gilpin Faust

A fascinating book about the terrible toll the war took on America. Not for those with weak stomachs—it can get a little grisly!

The Red Badge of Courage, by Stephen Crane

Fictional story of a young soldier struggling with his fear of battle. Total classic. A must-read. (And Beau's favorite book!)

The Killer Angels, by Michael Shaara

Historical novel about what went down at the real battle of Little Round Top. Warning: You may develop a raging crush on Tom Chamberlain. Or maybe that's just me. (Don't worry, Garrett, he's like two hundred years old!)

Civil War Cookbook, by William C. Davis

I wish we'd had more of these recipes this summer! History can be delicious—just avoid the salt pork.

So you've read all the books—the next step is to live it! Want to get involved in a Civil War reenactment? (Or maybe just visit one?) Everything you need to know here: www.reenactmenthq.com

acknowledgments

I feel like a second book needs twice as many thank-yous! Amanda Lewis, you are the Wonder Woman of agents, which makes Doe Coover the Justice League of agencies. Thank you for always being on my side. A big thank-you to everyone at HMH Graphia, especially Bethany Vinhateiro, the most brilliant editor *ever.* Thank you for loving these books as much as I do and helping to make them so much better.

My friends—the SatV girls, the Spice Girls, the Midd Girls, Caitlin, Evie, and Becky B—you guys are my biggest cheerleaders. Pepper, I hope we always have adventures together. To all my southern friends (War Eagle/Roll Tide), I hope I got it right. Max, I write love stories for a living, and I still don't have the words.

Mom, you are the best unofficial publicist a girl could ask for. Baby sister, without you I would have no blog material. Dad, we are like the literary version of Beyoncé and her dad, except I will never fire you.

Thanks to everyone who read *Pilgrims Don't Wear Pink*—without you, this book wouldn't exist! Thanks to all of my teachers, especially Ian Campbell and Amy Morsman. Finally, whoever digitized *Godey's Lady's Book,* you are my hero.

"Before He Cheats"